Keeping Hannah
Waiting

A Novel

Dave Clarke

Hologram Publishing

Hologram Publishing Cheyenne, WY

To Mom and Dad:

Thanks for showing me what true dignity is.

To Widge and Doobug:

Thanks for being who you are.

To Parts:

Thanks for all these years together,

you fill my world with love and joy everyday.

For the Survivors

Time slips away.

Eternally. Irretrievably.

Perpetually immersed in its sum and substance,

Yet it remains completely impalpable,

save when it's gone . . .

I

One

The late afternoon sunlight filtering through the attic
panes that day was, as always at this time of year, soft. Bright, yet
pale. Serene, yet crisp. This was the light master painters see in
their dreams; the light composers bathe in while they write their
greatest symphonies. This was the light Kate McBride liked to
remember her mother in. Here, where the good times were, the best
times.

"Mama," she whispered wistfully, sitting cross-legged on
the attic floor. She watched as motes of dust danced like tiny
snowflakes on the warm air currents in the broad shaft of light
spilling in the window. Her fingers tooled aimlessly along the
binding of a book she had plucked from one of the hundred or
more boxes bursting with volumes on every topic imaginable that
filled every cranny and corner of the home she had grown up in.
"Now that you've rescued all your other children," she said
looking out at the sea of books around her, "what am I supposed to
do with them? The libraries don't want them, I've asked. The
poor?" she continued, plucking another one at random.
"Apparently even they don't need another copy of *Vacuum Tubes,*
Radios of Tomorrow. No matter what Charles R. Shively or

Spectrum Publishing thought in 1927." Then she tossed the thin, technical thesis back onto the pile.

Kate—Kathleen Anne Quinlan McBride when she had gotten her mother's Irish up, Katie-dearest, to a father who had passed on too long ago and far too soon—took in the savory, sweet smell of papyrus that hung in the air up here as if it were her mother's own perfume, and, for the first time in her thirty-two years, she realized that, in a very real way, it was.

"There's no room for them in my tiny place. It's time they moved on too. I'm sorry, Mama... I'm sorry." Kate McBride stood up and wiped the tears from her eyes with the tissue clutched tightly in her hand. She smoothed her sweater down, then bent down to twist her pant leg straight. As she tugged at the denim, her elbow caught another literary brick, knocking it down, first along the narrow flight of stairs from the attic, then in two giant leaps, down the second flight, finally landing in the alcove in the front hallway. Kate sighed under her breath and followed slowly down the stairs after it, the last pinkish-yellow rays of sunshine drifting in through the attic window and lighting a path for her.

A burgundy, leather-bound book, about the size of a ledger, something about it felt good the moment Kate grasped it up in her hands off the hardwood floor. Engraved on the front, in a fanciful gothic font, a pair of gilded letters: *H.B.* Nothing else. Initials perhaps, she thought, as she caught sight of a tiny, frayed bit of cream-colored canvas thread sticking out of the worn, rounded spine.

She slid open the hardcover, its pages held together by the gluey potion of time and dust and, separating the sheets, Kate read the title leaf hand-inked in an old-school cursive in black fountain pen. *"Die Zu-las-sung,"* she struggled in a quiet whisper. *"Die Zulassung,"* she repeated. "1940. *Die Zulassung,* 1940... A collector whose passion knew no borders, huh Mama, whether you could understand a single word or not?" Shutting the volume, Kate McBride pressed the cover down, but catching sight of the frayed fragment of canvas again she opened the book once more and tried pressing it gently back into the spine. As she did, a few brightly colored pebbles sprinkled out, landing in a flurry of soft clicks on the wooden floorboards at her feet, where, she saw, they had joined up with a similarly colored tiny pile of confetti bits where the book landed after its tumblesome journey down the stairs.

Holding the old edition up to the first rays of moonlight beaming down now from the attic, Kate pulled the covers away and let the aged, yellowy pages inside dangle beneath in loose clumps. "Ohh," she whispered as she peeked inside the spine. "There's something in there."

Kate McBride worked the contents—a roll of canvas— inch by inch, until she had freed a scroll from the snug vellum sanctuary where, she reckoned, it had resided for half a century at least. Slowly, she unrolled the cloth until the image painted there revealed itself fully in the shaft of bluish-white light now streaming down from the heavens in giant waves through the attic window. "Sweet Jesus," she gasped.

Frozen, Kate stared at what she held in her now-trembling hands: a portrait, a work in oil of a young woman lying in a field of lavender. The face so pure, so perfect in form and proportion, that the hand of God, woven so inextricably into the whole of humanity, was revealed there instantly. Someone had come upon

3

an angel and captured her shining spirit for eternity in a brilliant flurry of brushstrokes.

Even muted in the layers of dust, the colors danced across the canvas. Kate lightly blew away the powder and the woman's eyes—two cornflower blue blossoms glistening in the noonday summer sun—still glittered with life. Sandy, blonde wisps of hair clung loosely around the slender frame of her high, tanned cheekbones, and, poised beneath a perfect nose—lips so pink, so full of life, they seemed to draw breath between them even now.

. . . .

Two

She had no idea how long she had been standing there in the entryway, but when Kate finally looked up, darkness and a thick fog had set in. That's it, she thought walking into the living room, I'm staying here. She had makeup, clean undies, and a spare uniform in the hall closet. And besides, this was closer to work in the morning.

But then, realizing she didn't want to sleep in her old bed, and she certainly didn't want to sleep in her mother's bed, Kate wasn't sure what to do. So she just sat down on the sofa, curled her legs up beneath her and pulled the quilt folded neatly there on the armrest across her lap, setting the portrait down beside her.

In the soft, creamsicle-colored glow of the streetlamp just outside her front window, Kate looked around at the room that was the center of her world for the first twenty years of her life. The blue-green area rug was the forest where she set up her dolls and the brick hearth across the room, the castle far, far away, she remembered with a smile. Across from that, the rocking chair where her mother had sat, hours on end, night after night, reading under the dim light that seeped out from the lamp tucked in the corner behind her.

And if she wasn't reading, then it seemed that Mary McBride was always fitting Kate in some costume, for a church play, or a school dance, or Halloween. She would stand on the coffee table in her bare feet while her mother transformed her into a fairy princess, or a ballerina, or Little Red Riding Hood. How many Halloweens, how many costumes, she thought back with a smile.

It was on this very couch, she remembered now, where one afternoon in seventh grade, her mother gone to some meeting, that Kate got her first kiss from Bobby Russo who lived three houses down. And come to think of it, this was also the site of her first breakup just a few months later. This was where she celebrated communion and graduation. Here, where a week later, she announced her job at the bakery, and two years after that, that she had saved enough money to take a place of her own.

She looked over at the window and watched as the condensation beaded up on the panes, then trickled down in ziggedy-zaggedy drips. The front window was where Mary McBride ushered in every holiday with a new display: hearts and lace doilies in the days leading up to Valentine's; pastel bunnies hopping alongside brightly colored eggs in the weeks prior to Easter. In October, it was ghosts and skeletons, followed by crepe paper turkeys in November, and immediately thereafter, by Santas, snowmen, and reindeer.

Just why her mother went to all that trouble Kate never understood, until that one day in high school she heard someone talking in a loud voice outside the window and she peeked out from behind the curtains. "Oopsies," she heard a woman say. "We forgot to wave hi to Santa." Then she watched as the woman wheeled the stroller she was pushing back around and parked it in front of the window, her bundled-up baby facing the display. "We can't go for our walk without saying hi to Santa, can we?" the young mother asked her child. Then she bent down next to the infant and waved and said, "Hi Santa. Hi Frosty. Hi Rudolph, hi Vixen, and Blitzen, and Dasher, and Donner." And in the instant Kate saw the baby wave hi and the pure, wholesome smile on its face—and the one just as joyous on the young mother—she understood why her mother did it year after year. She was planting smiles in people's hearts one by one as they passed her house.

Yes, she had a place of her own but it was here, in this small room, where Kate really learned about life. Not in some classroom, not from some sermon, but in these close, quiet quarters, and in the tiniest and most intimate ways. The really important lessons, the kind only a mother can teach a daughter—right from wrong, courage, compassion—those were taught stitch by stitch and page by page. Kate knew she was going to miss this place when it was gone.

Kate McBride peeled open one eye. She looked at the clock on the mantle, but she didn't have to. She knew what time it was. After twelve years of getting up at three-thirty every morning Kate didn't need an alarm. The only thing that puzzled her was how on Sundays, her body or her mind—she wasn't sure which—knew to sleep in until it was time to get up for church.

She looked down and confirmed that the object that had kept her awake all night, save perhaps the last hour—the painting—was still there beside her. Even in the moonlight that now filled the room with its bluish-white light, the woman's eyes were just as alive, her lips just as pink. "Who are you?" Kate

7

whispered hoarsely to the woman staring out at her so intensely from the canvas. "*Who* are you?"

She extracted herself from the rocker and walked into the downstairs bathroom. Then Kate McBride slipped out of her sweater and jeans, washed up, and pulled on the clean bra and panties she had plucked off the shelf in the hall cabinet. Then she took the pale-pink bakeshop uniform off the hanger on the bathroom door and she stepped into the garment, pulling the thin crinoline fabric down across her hips and twisting it straight before buttoning it up. As she did, Kate caught her reflection in the mirror on the closet door. At five-two, she had her mother's petite build. She also had Mary McBride's nose and her same, fair complexion lightly peppered with freckles. She had her mother's eyes too: two bouquets of heather with sparkling flecks of green. But her hair—thick, dark, reddish-brown locks that bobbed in soft, rich waves gently above her shoulders—that was all her father's. And the high cheekbones that gave way to a broad, engaging smile, those she also owed entirely to Thomas McBride.

When she was ready to leave, Kate walked back into the living room, picked up the painting, rolled it up, slipped it into a plastic bag, and slid a thin, blue rubber band over the top. Then she dropped the scroll and the leather book—H.B's meticulously maintained journal—gently into her purse. She put on her coat, turned out the lights, and locked the door behind her.

Others might mind having to get up so early, but not Kate. On days like this, with the winds whipping onshore from Sheepshead Bay and nothing, and no one, on the streets to stop them, the aromas from the bakery, just four blocks from the house, bounced off the brownstones like moonbeams in the cool, predawn air through her old neighborhood.

On misty mornings like this the streetlamps glowed like giant Tootsie Pops. In this light, the corner market seemed more Rockwell painting than rundown liquor store. Instead of diminishing whatever it touched, in this iridescent glow, the graffiti tucked into the alleyways and sprayed onto the fire hydrants and street signs added dimension and texture, and a certain raw energy.

By the time she pulled open the back door of the bakery and took her first, full, supersaturated, damp whiff of 350-degree bakery-rich air, Kate McBride sometimes couldn't tell whether she was just going to work or somehow symbolically returning to the womb. But, she had decided long ago, either way was fine and she pulled open the door, letting the hot air wash over her like a giant wave.

"Gooda morning, Katalina," Sal DeCicco said, his accent as thick as the black mustache planted between his big, Romanesque nose and his thick, full lips.

"Morning, Mr. D.," Kate answered, taking off her coat and purse and swapping them for the small, white apron hanging on the hook by the back door. "Morning, Mrs. D." she called out slipping the apron on over her head and heading for the front of the shop.

"*Buongiorno bambina*," Maria DeCicco called back from the storeroom.

"Did you see whatta he did yesterday, Katalina?" Sal DeCicco asked.

Sal didn't have to say who "he" was, Kate knew. "He" was whoever was in the White House at the time. "Yes, Mr. D., I saw," Kate said. To Sal, whoever was in the Oval Office was a bum who didn't know how to run the country. And, Kate had to admit with a smile, for the most part, he was right. The world probably would be a better place if someone with values as simple and honest as Salvatore DeCicco ran it.

With that little bit of politics taken care of, they went about their business. Kate ran the water for two pots of coffee, regular and decaf. Maria DeCicco pulled the brown paper bag with the cash for the till out from under the second sack of flour closest to the storeroom. Then, as Kate moved racks of ryes into the grated metal bins stacked on the counter behind the glass cases, Sal DeCicco worked in the back squeezing his sweet, chocolate chip-ricotta filling in quick, big sploshes from the pastry bag into the thin, crisp cannoli shells lined up in neat rows on baking pans on the long, marble countertop lining the back wall of the bakery.

Before she pulled the cord to switch on the neon sign that alternately flashed HOT then FRESH, then HOT again, in bright, orange-red in the front window, Kate McBride looked around to check that everything was in place and counted it out in her head: Cookies: two, four, six, eight kinds, she confirmed quickly. Cakes: one, two, three, four, five, six. Check. Danish: cheese, apple, cherry. Check. Rolls: sweet, sour, seeded and without, poppy and dinner. Done. Tarts: apple, berry, cheese, lemon, custard. All where they should be. The bins behind the shelves held the required half a dozen loaves each of sourdough, rye, Italian, white, wheat, and foccacia. She turned back to the front counter and reached over to pull open the lid of the numbers dispenser and checked to make sure there were enough paper service tickets on the roll to at least get them through the rush of customers that came every morning a few minutes before six when the Ave D line of the subway drew its first crowd of commuters looking for warm pastry and something hot to drink on the way into Penn Station.

With everything as it should be, Kate watched as Maria DeCicco placed the dollar bills in the register the same as always: first the ones, then the fives, tens, and twenties, her tiny fingers quickly flipping through the stacks of bills as she counted each one out twice in Italian under her breath, "*Una, due, tria…*"

When she was done, Kate said, "I want to show you something."

"What's that?" Maria asked, shutting the drawer.

"Stay right there," Kate said skipping out into the back room. When she came out a minute later with her bag, she saw a face in the window and changed course to open the front door first. She slipped the bag over her shoulder, rolled up the shade, switched on the HOT and FRESH sign, and then turned the latch on the door. "Hi sweetie," she told the little bundled up Brooklynite blowing in the door.

"That wind is something else, huh *chica*?" Connie Perez asked, clutching herself and shivering. She unwrapped her coat and scarf to reveal her petite size two frame, then brushed back her thick, black hair exposing her eyes, a pair of sapphire blue gems.

"Wasn't too bad when I came in," Kate answered, then walked back behind the glass case, and poured some steaming hot black coffee into a paper cup and set it down on the counter for her friend.

"Well, something's brewing out there, that's for sure," Connie Perez said, cupping her hands around the coffee and taking a small sip. "That's better," she sighed and took another small drink.

"Check this out," Kate said as she pulled the plastic bag out of her purse, sliding the rubber band off the top.

"Looka what?" Sal DeCicco coming out from the back, a tray of muffins resting on the shelf that was his white, doughy stomach.

Kate slipped the canvas out of the plastic, laid it on the glass countertop and unrolled it.

"Jesus, Mary, and Joseph," Connie Perez gasped.

"*Mamma mia*," Sal DeCicco said.

Maria DeCicco put one hand to her mouth and made the sign of the cross with the other.

Kate watched the three of them fall silent and spellbound under the portrait's powerful presence, just as she had the night before. They stood and stared, awe-stricken for quite some time, before Connie finally broke the silence and whispered, "She's… it's…beautiful."

"*Bellisima*," Maria barely got out.

"*Bella, tre bella*," Sal said faintly, shaking his head and twirling his mustache.

"Where'd you get it?" Connie Perez asked, regaining her composure.

"I was in Mama's attic last night trying to figure out what to do with all those books and I knocked one of them down the stairs by accident. This one," Kate McBride said, pulling the small journal from her bag. "It was rolled up in here," she explained, wiggling her finger into the spine.

Sal DeCicco took the book from her and looked at it. "*Die Zulassung.* 1940," he said and began flipping open the pages. "German," he said bluntly.

"It's amazing," Connie continued, still in awe. "I don't think I've ever seen anything like it."

"Do you know what that means, *Die Zulassung?*" Kate asked the baker.

"No, I justa recognize some of the words. *Vassar, tzein litres,*" he offered. "Water, ten liters. I remember a little German from the war, but I never spoke it. It looksa like some kind of a record book, though."

"What are you going to do with it?" Connie asked.

"I don't know," Kate mused. "It must belong to someone. To H.B., probably, whoever he or she was. Or his heirs if he has any. I think it's a he…" Kate continued, turning the pages of the journal slowly. "The handwriting is too stiff to be a woman's, in any language. But, either way, I have no idea where to begin. The police, I suppose."

"What if you can't find the owners? What if it's like this really rare painting and it's worth millions?" Connie Perez asked.

Kate raised her eyebrows sarcastically.

"It could happen," Connie postulated, then added warmly, "Boy, you look like your mama when you make that face." Then, picking up her coffee and walking toward the door, she added, "I'm gonna be a little late tonight, sweetie. Mrs. Mazzetti's coming in at 5:30 and no matter how blue I make her hair, it's never right.

She gets so bent out of shape, you'd swear the woman was cutting a video. See ya."

"See ya," Kate volleyed back.

"Oh, one more thing," Connie Perez said, one foot out the door. "Don't forget me when you're rich. Ten carats for this hand, and ten more over here so I'm not lopsided," she said wiggling her long, glittery, classic Brooklyn-hairdresser nails at Kate, who lobbed a sugar cookie at her in response.

"Get out of here," Kate joked, only half-laughing as the cookie shattered when it hit the front door.

"Hi, Mrs. K.," the hairdresser told the old woman shuffling into the bakery as she left.

"Good morning," the woman answered politely.

"Mrs. Klein, hi," Kate said.

"Ahhh…" the woman said taking a deep breath of the sweet, warm air in the bakery. "If I could just take this smell and put it in my house, I would never leave."

"How's Mr. Klein?"

"His eyes are itching him, his hip is acting up, and he's complaining about his lumbago. In other words," the woman said picking up a plastic bag of bow-tie twist cookies from the shelf, "he's fine."

"That's good," Kate said, rolling up the painting and dropping it back into the plastic bag and her purse, setting it under the register.

. . . .

Three

Andrew F. Rothman, Ph.D., Kate read on the faded, black plastic nameplate, then underneath, Chairman, Art Department. The nameplate held down a scruffy stack of papers on the professor's cluttered desk and Kate wondered briefly, what the "F." stood for. She waited and watched as the man looked over the painting, first with his round, gold-rimmed spectacles on, then with them off, then on again, gnawing on a pencil as he did.

Kate wanted to ask a million questions but she didn't want to sound foolish, so she limited herself to just one. "Do you know what that means?" she probed as Rothman picked up the leather journal and began leafing through it.

"*Die Zulassung,*" he said thoughtfully. "The logbook, if I remember my high school German correctly."

"Oh...." Kate acknowledged. "And have you heard of this painter, this Chay-gal? Is that how you pronounce it?" Kate McBride wanted to know.

The man didn't answer at first, his attention focused back on the portrait, that radiant face staring up at him from the square patch of frayed canvas holding him as mesmerized as everyone else who soaked those eyes in. Then, his mouth curled up at the edges into a thin smile, the crow's feet around his eyes deepened, and Andrew F. Rothman, Ph. D.'s sallow cheeks stretched across his bony face. "Chagall," he said in low voice. "Cha-gall," he enunciated. "Yes, I've heard of him," he continued, smiling warmly at the portrait.

"It's worth something then?" Kate McBride asked, instinctively trying to clutch the canvas back without seeming distrustful.

"I teach Introduction to Art History at Brooklyn Community College, Ms. McBride. I'm hardly an expert. I have no idea if it's genuine. But if it is…" he said, swiveling around on his chair, "I don't hesitate to say it's probably worth… a fortune.

"Providing that, as you suggest, no one else has claim to it," the professor theorized, "you could be a very, very, rich woman," he said rather matter-of-factly. Then he added in a somber tone, "Very," as if trying to etch the comprehension of fabulous wealth directly inside her skull.

"There, there. You're going to be fine, Ms. McBride," the professor told Kate, propping her up in the chair and tipping a glass of water to her lips. "You fainted. I suppose I'd collapse too if I'd just found out I might be worth several million dollars more than I was just moments earlier."

Kate began to sense composure settling back in over her and sat up.

"So, as I was saying, if this is an authentic Marc Chagall—and judging by the date here, 1910, it's apparently one of his earliest pieces—it could bring five or ten million dollars at auction. Maybe more. And if no one has title to it, well then, the first commandment of international cultural law applies."

Kate McBride stared at him, puzzled.

"Finders keepers," he laughed.

. . . .

Four

As she waited on the soft leather couch in the stylish reception area, Kate McBride thought back. The last time she was in this building, the Museum of Modern Art, was probably in the fifth grade. With Mrs. Nelson's class, she reminded herself as she searched her memory. Some boy had tried to put his hand up her blouse in a dark corner of the museum. Johnny... Johnny Somebody, she tried recalling unsuccessfully. It startled her then when a well-dressed man in his early sixties approached her and introduced himself.

"Ms. McBride? I'm Henry Placer, the acquisitions director here at MOMA. Please come in," he continued, leading her into his office. "Can I offer you anything? Some tea, coffee, a glass of water?" Henry Placer offered as he settled in behind his clear glass and steel desk.

"No, thank you," Kate answered, feeling more than a little out of sorts in this highbrow environment.

"How can I help you?"

"Professor Rothman, over at the college, Brooklyn Community, that is... " she explained, a slight edge in her voice. "He said you might be able to tell me if this is worth anything," Kate said, twisting the end cap off the mailing tube she now kept the painting in and slid the work out. "If it's real, you know, genuine, authentic," she offered nervously, handing over the canvas. "And..." she continued, "if anyone lost it or reported it stolen, that kind of thing."

"Well, let's see what we have," he said in a syrupy tone that seemed to have already appraised and dismissed the item based solely on Kate McBride's tweedy, frayed, top coat. "You indicated on the telephone you picked this up where, at a flea market?" he remarked smugly, unwinding the scroll.

"Probably, yes. I mean my mother probably did. She liked those sorts of things, garage sales, mini-storage auctions, you know."

"Yes, of course," he mocked her dryly.

Then, Kate McBride watched as the pieces of Henry Placer's face rearranged themselves, executing a clumsy u-turn from callous derision and continuing all the way around to respectful sobriety.

"How... how can I contact your mother?" the curator whispered, the lines in his face frozen in awe now.

"With a really good psychic, I suppose," Kate said without skipping a beat, savoring the upper hand she could see she had just gained. She watched Henry Placer search for the meaning in her reply. "She's dead. My mother passed about two months ago. I was cleaning out the attic in her house, my house, the house where I grew up over in Flatbush.

"You see," she explained further, "my mother rescued books. Anywhere and everywhere she found them. Out of dumpsters, recycling bins. That," she said pointing to the canvas now quivering in Placer's hand, "was rolled up inside this." Then, Kate McBride reached down and pulled the little leather volume from her bag. "In here," she pointed out, fingering the binding.

Placer quietly cleared a spot on his desk and lay the Chagall down setting four felt-bottomed paperweights at each of the corners to hold it open. He then took the book from Kate and pulled open its cover, carefully turning the yellowed leafs, studying them briefly, one by one. "German. At the beginning of the war," he mused to himself quietly as he got lost momentarily in the stiffly scripted text. "Seems like a logbook or something. 15 September 1940. 22 November... I don't know what it says," he told her, focusing his eyes again on the angelic face peering up at him from his desk. "Who else knows about this?" he wanted to know.

"It's real, then?"

He hesitated, then answered with a look revealing far more than his two brief words, "Quite possibly," could ever do, and Kate McBride smiled.

It was only two month's since Kate's aunt had passed away and finding herself emptying another set of cupboards into cardboard boxes didn't sit well with her. Why did these things always have to happen around the holidays, she wanted to know. And if they always come in threes, what was next?

"So, he's never heard of this painting before?" Connie asked as Kate stood on top of the step stool and handed down pieces of china to be wrapped in newspapers and set in the waiting boxes.

"No. But, he said generally speaking, the signature looks good and the brush strokes look right. But he's not a Chagall expert, that's how you pronounce it by the way—Sha-gahl," she explained. "Anyway, he's not aware of any outstanding claims for a missing Chagall matching this one, but he's going to put me in touch with the right people next week. There's museum people, auction house people, university people. There's even a group in Paris that helps make sure these things, Chagalls, are real. And there's another group in London that does nothing but reunite artwork that was looted, lost, or stolen during World War II with their original owners and vice versa. They're going to run some tests. We'll see."

In the harsh florescent light Connie Perez peered down through the spine of yet another book stashed up in cabinet between the teacups and the saucers. "You never know," she said smiling and handing it down to Kate who used it to top off another box full of books in the sea of packing boxes surrounding them. "It wouldn't be the first time lightning struck somewhere twice."

Still hanging on the kitchen walls were the clippings and snapshots of Mary McBride's very full life: a certificate of appreciation from the fourth grade PTA hung in a plain black frame next to a cluster of photos; Mary at the beach with friends; taking a third curtain call with the all-Girl Scout cast of "Annie" she directed; with the church choir; with the mayor, with a very young Bobby Kennedy at the foot of the Brooklyn Bridge. Always smiling, always at the center of it all, Mary McBride's list of accomplishments was long.

"Your mother was amazing," Connie said looking over all the memorabilia. "She did so much. It's almost like she was everywhere."

"She *was* everywhere," Kate McBride explained, then thought to herself, everywhere but here.

21

"Hey, how long will those tests take, you know, to prove if the painting is real or not?"

"A couple of weeks if there are no hang-ups."

"And then...?"

"I have to post notices in the papers around the world."

"And then?"

"If nobody comes along... it's like the professor said," Kate McBride continued. "But it's never gonna happen. Not to me, anyway. Somebody will come along to claim it. If you owned one of this guy's paintings and he's so famous and all, wouldn't you put out an all-points bulletin?

Climbing down from the stool, Connie asked a question Kate didn't have an answer for, "So why hasn't anybody?"

The question gave her pause, then Kate answered. "This is somebody's mother or daughter, or granddaughter. They should have it." With that, they continued packing in silence until soon, Kate began to sob.

"What's the matter, sweetie?" Connie asked anxiously, and then looking at her, took Kate in her arms, and held her friend tight.

"I'm... I'm not anybody's little girl anymore," Kate said, burrowing deeper into Connie's shoulder and letting it all out.

"I know, baby. I know." Connie said tenderly. "But it'll be alright. It's the way of the world. It was her time."

. . . .

Five

"**May I get you anything?**" Henry Placer asked in a strong voice, taking Kate's coat.

"No, thank you."

"This is Dr. Ernesto Montoya, the chair of Modern Art History at Columbia University, Monsieur Michel Favier, director of the Louvre Special Collections, Alastair Robinscourt with Sotheby's, Sarah Weinthorp with the Chagall Committee, and Anne Webber from the Commission for Looted Art in Europe."

"*Enchanté, mademoiselle,*" the Frenchman offered warmly, the others' salutations following politely after.

"You came all the way from Paris?" Kate McBride asked, impressed.

"A month ago. But had I not been here, I assure you, I would've come anyway, on the very next plane. May we be permitted?" he asked anxiously.

"Oh, of course," Kate said, slightly embarrassed at how tightly she was clutching the tube. "Here," she offered, handing it over to him.

Michel Favier extricated the swatch of canvas from its cylindrical home. The others gathered behind him as he brought the face to light. Those four people in the room who had never seen the painting before, let out a collective gasp as they first caught sight of the work. But then, they pulled out their

23

magnifying tools and began scouring the artist's handiwork with the most critical of eyes.

Each worked a different corner. Alastair Robinscourt assessed the fibers of the canvas itself, how they were wound, how they had been clipped from the loom. Anne Webber looked for the artist's markings on the backside of the canvas, prodding at them gently with a steel prong in search of how they had been made and in what order. Meanwhile Ernesto Montoya studied the composition itself, the balance and flavor of the colors, how they blended, contrasted, and bound the image together, and Michel Favier traced each curve, dip, and stroke of the signature with his jeweler's loupe in search of the slightest discrepancy in its formation and shape.

After a time, the activity subsided and the group set down their instruments and retracted their inspectors' claws. Kate was exhausted simply from the watching and anticipating. As Michel Favier approached, her back stiffened and her eyes widened, and the breath was slowly drawn out of her.

"Amongst the very elite of us," Favier began slowly in his French accent, "in the very innermost circles, there has long been talk about a portrait known simply as Girl with Flowers. In some of his letters Monsieur Chagall discusses a girl with flowers, but his grammatical taxonomy was never clear enough to allow us to determine whether he's speaking merely of someone he's seen on the street, or someone—and something—much more significant."

"One thing is clear," Robinscourt added precisely, "at right about this point in Chagall's life and career—1910, just before he got to Paris the first time—something significant happened. From this point forward, his growth as an artist is very

24

apparent. His work takes on an almost magical, childlike quality compared with the somber, more realistic tone of his earlier work. It's as if his imagination has been set free. Suddenly his images begin to float, his palette has broadened, and we start to see the bright blues and yellows and greens that became his trademark colors beginning to appear. Pinks and cherry reds start showing up where once there were only grays and browns."

"But," Sarah Weinthorp said in a serious tone, "Girl with Flowers has never been mentioned outside this circle for fear that the very mention of it—when none of us had ever actually seen it or even a picture of it—would in and of itself create an opportunity to fabricate a hollow image, a fake. But we all knew that if it surfaced on its own, and it had all the right markings, we would know in an instant it was genuine. And, although we need to confirm a few things in the laboratory, it appears... that's what we have here," the expert said somewhat breathless herself, in the end.

. . . .

Six

"Can you believe this place?" Connie Perez said, nudging Kate. "Look at these people," she gawked, surveying the well-heeled crowd gathered in Sotheby's Park Avenue auction house.

"Cut it out," Kate McBride protested nervously.

"Honey, these people got money to spend and they are dressed up to part with some serious cash tonight. Would you look at that one?" Connie asked, pointing at a society matron dripping with diamonds.

"Don't point," Kate corrected.

"If you wanted to put one more diamond on that woman you'd have to stick it—"

Before Connie's observation could make itself completely apparent, the auctioneer's gavel crackled crisply in the air three times and the auctioneer called the boisterous crowd to order. "Ladies and gentlemen, if you please. Thank you. Thank you, welcome to Sotheby's."

"I am so nervous," Kate told Connie, clutching her friend's hand tightly.

"What's there to be nervous about? Getting rich? Poor, I could understand. But rich, rich has gotta be much easier to take."

"I just feel like there's something I missed."

"For the one hundredth time," Connie Perez pleaded. "Everyone has checked out every possibility backwards and forwards: museums and galleries on every continent, insurance records, war records, you name it. And you and I have been to so many Jewish temples and agencies that if we had to go to one more, I swear, we'd have to get bat mitzvahed. Would you relax? It's yours. This money is going to be yours. It's *already* yours," she stated flat out.

"I just have this feeling that something's not right, something's been overlooked."

Suddenly, a puzzled look crossed Connie Perez's smooth, cocoa butter-colored face, and in a serious tone she said, "Oh my God... maybe we did." Then, she added with a smile, "But there's no way, *they* did," as she pointed out the Gang of Five, as they had come to call the experts, Montoya, Favier, Robinscourt, Webber, and Placer, over the past few months. "Yoo-hoo, hi," she waved at them across the room. "You know they've had everyone of their thousand-dollar-an-hour experts go over this deal with a fine-tooth comb. They're not gonna lay out that kind of dough, any one of them, let alone all of them, if this weren't solid."

"I guess," Kate McBride said weakly.

"We have many exciting pieces from a number of different collections for you this evening," the auctioneer began in his perfectly round, polished British tones. "We also have a number of guests on the phones joining us this afternoon from London and Paris," he said, acknowledging the house's representatives attending the phones with a nod and getting one back from them in return. "Let's get started, shall we? We begin with Lot number 75, Toothpaste, the petite Warhol from 1963,

27

from the collection of Mr. Felix Thorndike." The stagehands brought out an easel and set it under the spotlight. "This is on page 19 of your catalogs, an extraordinary piece which hasn't been on the market in more than 20 years," the auctioneer said as the drape covering the painting was pulled away.

Kate watched as the crowd settled down and the dollars began flying.

"Who will give me two? Two million dollars? Two million from the gentleman at the back. Do I have two million five? Two million five? Two million five hundred thousand dollars from the lady in the red hat. Thank you, madam. Do I have three? Three million in the front. A wise move, sir. We're talking Andy Warhol, ladies and gentlemen. Who will give me four? Four million on the phone from London, thank you bidder. Five, do I have five? If it doesn't find a new home this evening, I'm told this piece will not likely show up at market for another decade at least. Five million. Thank you sir. Six, do I have six? Will someone give me six? Is that it then? Five million. Going once. Five million, twice. Sold," he declared, bringing the gavel down with a sharp bang. "Five million dollars to the gentleman with the blue cravat. Congratulations, sir."

"Oh my god," Kate McBride said, flushed and out of breath.

"And if that went for five times what they said it would in the catalog, honey, you're in for a mighty fine night," Connie Perez told her friend. "That little, bitty Warhol is nowhere near as important a piece as yours."

"I'm getting nervous."

"Getting?" Connie asked sarcastically as she looked down at Kate's hands trembling in her own. "Shh, look they're bringing yours out."

"Next up, from the cover of our catalog, the star, the grande dame of the evening, Lot 102, the often-whispered, but until recently never seen, 'Girl with Flowers,' by the great Russian-French master, Marc Zakharovich Chagall," the auctioneer explained as the easel took its place at center stage. "As far as is known, ladies and gentlemen, this is the first time this piece has ever been to market. From the estate of Mary Elizabeth McBride and Kathleen Anne McBride, I give you 'Girl with Flowers,'" he crowed. As the drape covering the painting was whisked off, the angelic face on the canvas worked its magical charms yet again, producing one gigantic, collective gasp from the audience.

"Look at that," Connie said, elbowing Kate with a smile. "You already got your own estate."

"Stunning, isn't she?" the auctioneer declared. "This is one of the master's earliest works, done long before he was spirited out of southern France by the French resistance in 1940. Except to know that in 1910, Monsieur Chagall was en route from his tiny native Vitebsk in Belorussia to Paris, we have no knowledge of precisely where this work was done, or who the subject of this glorious painting is. It was around this time in Chagall's career, when the painter made his 'great lyrical explosion, his triumphant entry into modern painting,' as Andre Breton noted in his 1941 tribute. Perhaps looking at this exquisite angel, now we finally know why. The period that followed, through 1914, was indeed Chagall's most prolific.

"And of all the themes he explored, from life in his beloved Vitebsk to his uncle—the original fiddler on the roof, to the bible, the circus, and the world of dreams, one stood out above all the rest. And, for all the colors of the rainbow he painted with, from the unmistakable Chagallian blues to his rich reds, bold yellows, and vibrant greens, one stood out above all the rest. And in the master's mind, they were one and the same. 'There is but one single color that gives meaning to life and art,' Chagall said, 'the color of love.' And Girl with Flowers certainly demonstrates that, does she not?" the auctioneer declared in a strong voice. "Well, shall we have at it, then ladies and gentlemen? Judging by your earlier reaction, we'll pay no heed whatsoever to the reserve. Who will give me five million dollars?"

"Relax," Connie cautioned, grabbing on to a flush Kate. "Breathe deep. Everything's gonna be fine."

"Five million, thank you madam."

"Six, a voice at the back of the room shouted.

"Seven," another chimed in.

"Thank you Do I have eight? Eight million down in front. Nine. Nine on the aisle. Do I have ten? Ten million dollars on the phone from London. Who'll give me twelve?"

"Twelve," a voice called out.

"Fifteen," Henry Placer announced.

"Ladies and gentlemen, this is perhaps the most important find in a generation at least, one of the earliest pieces from an absolute giant of twentieth century painting. This truly is one of the rarest of rare opportunities to ever come along. I have fifteen, who will give me twenty?"

"Twenty," some shouted.

30

"We have twenty-five on the telephone from Paris," the auctioneer acknowledged quickly. "Do I have thirty? You won't likely see this item for sale again for a generation at least."

"Thirty million," the woman in the red hat said.

"We have thirty million. Do I have thirty-five? We have thirty million, going once. Thirty million twice– "

Thirty-five million dollars," someone called from the aisle.

"We have thirty-five, who will give me forty? Forty million dollars for something as exquisite as this, it's a bargain," the auctioneer suggested without a hint of sarcasm. "There it is, forty million on the phone from London. Do I have forty-five? Forty-five million for Girl with Flowers?"

"Fifty million dollars," Michel Favier called out from his place at the side of the room.

"Bravo, sir. Well done. Fifty million dollars from the gentlemen representing La Louvre. Will anyone give me more? Fifty-one? Then, fifty million going once. Fifty million going twice. There she is, ladies and gentlemen. Look at those angel eyes." And with a report as crisp as any pistol, he slammed the down the gavel. "Sold! The Girl with Flowers will have new home in La Louvre for fifty million dollars."

With that, Connie fainted dead away into Kate McBride's waiting arms. "You were right, Mama. There *is* something valuable in every book," Kate whispered to herself, smiling and clutching the leather-bound logbook in her hand.

· · · ·

31

Seven

"What are *you* doing here?" Connie asked Kate in the pre-dawn light as she walked into DeCicco's the next morning.

"What do you mean, what am I doing here?" Kate answered. "What does it look like I'm doing? I'm working," she said impatiently, continuing to set out the fresh baked goods and pouring Connie's coffee.

"Do I really need to point this out to you? Hello-o-o? Do you remember last night at all? You don't need to work again. *Ever!*"

"Hello-o-o," Kate mimicked. "I know that, but that doesn't mean I don't have responsibilities. What am I supposed to do? Call the DeCicco's at midnight and say, 'Sorry, I'm too rich to come in tomorrow morning, you're on your own? Besides, I told you, I don't want anybody else to know yet. I don't want people getting all weird on me. Hey, you didn't tell anybody did you? You told. Who did you tell?"

"Who could I tell between last night and now, which, by the time you polished off that last glass of champagne, was only three hours ago? I'm gonna have a helluva day," Connie Perez lamented, rubbing her forehead. "Why did I let you talk me into all that champagne?"

"*I* talked *you* into all that champagne? I was the one who finally said to go home at two a.m.."

32

"Potato, potahto," Connie Perez said, grabbing a Danish and dropping two dollars on the counter as she headed for the door. "Are we still good for tonight?"

"Tonight? What's tonight? Oh, the ball game. Yeah, no, wait. I'm meeting the real estate agent at my mother's house at 7:00."

"You're still selling the house?"

"Yeah, why not?"

"I don't know. You don't need to sell it anymore, do you?"

"No…but I don't need it either. I mean, I don't want it. What am I going to do with it?"

"I don't know. But now at least you have an opportunity to decide if you *want* to sell it, not just sell it because you have to."

"I suppose you're right," Kate McBride conceded.

"Girl, I'm always right. Didn't I tell you that you were going to be rich one day? And…?"

"I don't know what to do," Kate said in low voice. "This changes everything. The money changes everything."

"Well, there are a few decisions you've got to make now. Like what to do with the rest of your life. In the meantime, just call me about tonight. Before lunch," Connie said, then dashed out of the bakery.

"The rest of my life," Kate muttered under her breath. "Oh right, that."

. . . .

33

"So, you're gonna move, right?" Connie, asked, standing there in her Yankees hat and jacket as Kate opened the door to her apartment to let her in. "I mean, when you got money Flatbush ain't exactly your first choice, is it?"

"Can you stop that, please?" Kate McBride pleaded gently. "Can we not talk about money for just one minute?"

"Okay, Okay, chill out. I'm sorry," Connie said, brushing past her in the doorway.

Kate McBride's second floor walk-up was the opposite of her mother's house in every possible way. The scant pieces of Kate's life —a high school graduation picture with her parents, the Empire State Building an inch and a half tall, encased in a water-filled clear plastic bubble, a worn, button-nosed teddy bear—were neatly organized, each in their proper place.

"I'm sorry," Kate said, changing her tone. "I'm a little edgy is all. I don't know what to do. I know it sounds crazy. I know I can do anything I want, but I have no idea what that is. There's a million thoughts going through my mind every second. It's making me nuts."

"Who says you *have* to do anything? Certainly not right away," Connie Perez said as they moved into Kate's tiny kitchen. "One of the things money buys you is the time and the right to do nothing at all. You've got time now, take it. Give notice at DeCicco's and then just take some time for yourself. Two weeks, three weeks, a month, six months, whatever. Figure out what you want to do. Make a plan and then go do it. Live your dreams. Do you know how many millions, no, hundreds of millions, billions, of people, dream about being able to do that?"

Kate McBride thought about it for a moment. "Maybe you're right."

"Maybe?" Connie said with a smug grin. "And to do it properly, you need a change of scenery. How can you possibly know what in the whole, entire world you want to do, where you want to be, unless you've at least seen something past 189th Street? You need to go see what's out there, girl. There must be life beyond the Verrazano Bridge, I'm sure of it."

The idea slowly seeped into Kate McBride's mind and she said, "You know, you might be right. I don't have to do anything right away and I've always wanted to travel. That'll give me time to sort some things out."

"Are we going to the game or what?" Connie asked.

"I can't go to the game now. You go without me. You don't mind, do you? Lizzie and Fran will be there. You guys'll have a good time. Tell them I had a cold. Send them my best. I'll see you in the morning, okay?"

. . . .

"Come on, Consuelo, hurry up and get here already," Kate McBride pleaded to herself as she paced back and forth, putting another rack of cookies out in the early morning light. "Connie. *Come on.*"

It took a few minutes, but her pleas were answered and Connie Perez walked through DeCicco's front door and headed straight for the coffee pot behind the counter.

"Europe," Kate blurted out.

"What?" a half-asleep Connie Perez asked in a throaty voice.

"Europe. I want to go to Europe," Kate burst out, showing her the pages of a travel brochure. "We land in London and spend a week in England. Shakespeare, Robin Hood, Buckingham Palace. Then, on to Paris. Four days in the City of Lights. From there we board a riverboat and cruise into the French countryside, down the Rhine Valley through Germany, and into Italy. Milan, Florence, Rome, and then we end up in Athens. There are planes and boats and trains and carriage rides too. *Carriage rides*, can you believe it? We leave two weeks from Saturday."

"We? Who's we?" Connie Perez asked.

"What do you mean 'Who's we?' You and me is we. Us. We're we."

"I don't have that kind of money. And, no, you're not paying for me. If you don't want the money to change things between us, then don't start with this. Besides, I can't leave the shop for a month, you know that."

"Gina can make Mrs. Mazzetti's hair look like blueberry cotton candy for once."

"That may be, but this trip is about *you*. You need to do this by yourself. Think things through on your own."

"I know that, but I don't want to go by myself. It's no fun. Come with me for a little while, say the first two weeks, then you can come back, and I can stay on and sort things out if I have to. It's like you said, I've got the rest of my life. You can pay for yourself, for the plane fare anyway. You can share a room with me, can't you, that won't change things will it? And, how about this? Breakfast on you, dinner on me, and we split lunch?"

Connie Perez just smiled and gave Kate a warm hug. Then the two of them jumped up and down screaming like teenage girls at a boy-band pop concert. "We're going to Europe! We're going to Europe!"

. . . .

Eight

"I am so nervous," Kate McBride confessed, her hands trembling as she tried buckling her seat belt.

"*You're* nervous?" Connie snapped back. "Sweetie, if you pinch me and this turns out to be real, I swear I'll pee right here in my pants just like I did in fifth grade when Bobby Russioli tried to feel me up at the back of the bus on the way home from that planetarium field trip. Do you remember that? My god, I was so embarrassed I don't think I went back to school for a week," she said all in one breath. Then, after a beat, Connie Perez said stubbornly, "I can't believe you upgraded me to first class without asking. I thought we agreed on who pays what and no splurging."

"Relax, there wasn't any splurging. It turns out that books weren't the only thing Mama started collecting when Daddy died. She had her fair share of frequent flyer miles too," Kate said, smiling and waving Mary McBride's Platinum MileSaver card before putting it in her purse.

"Well, it's a good thing for you coach and business class are full or I'd make you suffer up here alone," Connie said with a laugh.

Kate McBride continued fidgeting with her seatbelt, until suddenly, a pair of well-groomed man's hands gently took hers and in one deft move, guided the flat metal tip into the buckle with a snap.

"There you go, Ms. McBride," the steward said in his crisp British accent. "May I bring you anything?" Then, looking over at Connie, "Ms. Perez? Would you care for some coffee, tea? Wine, perhaps? A juice or sparkling water? I'll bet I know just the thing," he said. Then he turned and, stopping another attendant as she passed by, took two flutes of champagne from her tray, each centered on a small, gold-rimmed china saucer with a ripe, red strawberry nearly the size of an apple wedged atop the glass. He set them down on the white linen cloth covering the center armrest between Connie. "Cheers," he said, then turned and went on to the next passenger.

"Cheers to you and your cute little British behind too," Connie Perez joked after he was out of earshot.

Then, Kate McBride watched out her window as the Manhattan skyline faded from view and the jet glided in a wide arc through the dusky sky, eclipsing everything but the vast, blue expanse of Atlantic below and the puffy, white clouds that passed by in front of her now in foggy waves like subway trains before they disappeared into the inky sky behind her.

"You miss her, huh baby?" Connie Perez asked as she looked over at her friend.

Completely engrossed in an old snapshot of herself and her mother at a swim meet, Kate said, "Huh? No, what? I was going through my bag and I must've gotten distracted. What did you say?"

"Never mind," Connie said, then, "Oh, hey." Bending down, she picked up a stick of lipstick from the cabin floor. "Here," she said handing it to Kate. "This must've fallen out."

"Thanks. I swear there's a hole in that purse, but I can't find it." Then turning her attention back to the picture, Kate McBride said, "I couldn't have been more than seven here, maybe seven and a half. She used to judge our competitions. She really liked swimming."

"What about you?"

"What about me?" Kate McBride asked in a disinterested voice.

"Did you like it?" her friend prodded.

"It was okay, I guess. I mean everybody should know how to swim, right?"

"Right," Connie agreed. Then, changing her tone, she added, "It almost looks like you two are in different pictures."

Kate didn't answer, except to mentally chide herself for thinking, 'We might as well have been.'

Changing gears, Connie Perez took a sip of cognac and asked, "What's on the agenda for tomorrow?"

"Let's see," Kate said, pulling a brochure out of her bag and unfolding it on her lap. "London, Day One," she read aloud. "In the morning, after our Continental breakfast we make our way to Westminster Abbey where the kings and queens of England have been crowned for over four hundred years. From there we're off to Buckingham Palace to see the changing of guards, then lunch and over to the Tower of London for a peek at the Crown Jewels before we have high tea at Harrods at four. Then, dinner at the restaurant of our choice and we're whisked away in a London cab to see the world's longest-running stage production, Agatha Christie's "The Mousetrap" in the West End Theater."

"That's it? Palaces, cathedrals, kings, queens, and the Crown Jewels?" Connie Perez asked sarcastically. "That's the best you can do? I gotta pee," she said in her abrupt way, then snapped open her seat belt and headed for the lavatory.

England in the summertime was every bit the fairy tale Kate McBride always imagined it to be. To her, London seemed a Dickens novel come to life, and the dewy, green countryside was full of the pleasure of life in every breath. Lurking around every bend in the road was the possibility of a chance encounter with Robin, Arthur, or Maid Marian. Under its spell and the irresistible forces of her first foreign excursion, Kate soon sensed in herself the transformations a change in landscape inevitably brings, and she began to succumb to those feelings quite voluntarily now.

"Not that you need it, but a penny for your thoughts," Connie asked as they strolled through the heart of Shakespeare's Stratford-upon-Avon.

"The same thoughts I've had ever since I got that check from the auction house, only more often now. What did I do to deserve this money? Isn't there somebody else who could use it more? What should I do now? Technically, the book belonged to my mother. What would she do with the money?"

"What about this and what about that?" Connie Perez chided. "What if you just accept the facts? By a stroke of dumb luck, call it the grace of God if you like, your mother paid a dime for a book that happened to contain a painting worth fifty million dollars. She didn't even know she had it. When she passed away, you inherited it along with all the rest of her possessions. And most of that stuff, pardon me, was worthless junk, just like in a million other basements and attics around the world. You did everything to find a rightful owner. Twice, for chrissakes. Maybe once, just once in life, the good girl really does win. Is that possible?"

Kate McBride didn't answer.

"You know what I think this is really all about?" Connie continued. "You think that no matter what you do with the money you're afraid it won't be good enough in your mother's eyes. Or what you *think* is good enough in your mother's eyes."

"What?!" Kate McBride huffed.

"Don't give me that. You know exactly what I mean. I'm sorry to say this, but nothing you ever did was good enough for your mother."

"How could it be? My mother was the head of the PTA; I was the kid expelled from the school. My mother was the president of the women's church league; I was practically excommunicated."

"You turned out pretty darn good in my book."

"I was a disappointment."

"Then I guess the two of you are even," Connie told her friend bluntly, then walked ahead.

Nine

At the Louvre, the Mona Lisa's half-smile still beguiling all comers, Connie Perez asked, "Where do you think they'll put your painting?"

Before Kate could answer, a male voice with a thick French accent approached them from behind and said smoothly, "I will show you exactly where."

Kate and Connie turned around to find Michel Favier. "Mademoiselle McBride, why didn't you let us know you were coming? We could have prepared a special welcome for you. Ah, but no matter, I am delighted you're here. Welcome. And *bienvenue aussi*, Ms. Perez, it's a pleasure to see you again as well. You must let me be your guide to La Louvre," Favier said cheerfully. "I insist," he emphasized and then, using his cell phone, advised his staff of his new-found plans.

They moved from masterwork to masterwork, Favier patiently and lovingly explaining the history and significance of each piece until long after every other visitor had been escorted from the building. "Well, that was our little museum, or at least the highlights... with one exception of course," Favier added with a smile. Then he turned and pointed to an alcove, a space blocked off from public view by a long, royal blue velvet curtain, and a small hand-lettered sign that said, '*En route, Chagall, Fille avec Fleurs.*' Then below, in English, Coming: Chagall, Girl with Flowers. "This is where she will reside," the curator said, pulling the drape back to reveal the workspace in progress. "We are preparing this place especially for her so she will have the light for the, how do you say it in English, *le coucher du soleil*... ah yes, for the sunset," he said pointing to the skylights above. "Just as she was when Monsieur Chagall painted her."

"It's beautiful," Kate McBride said firmly and meant it.

"Very nice," Connie agreed, peeking in.

Favier glanced down at his wristwatch. "*Mon dieu*, look at the time. *Mademoiselles*, do you have plans for the dinner? May I have the pleasure of your company this evening?"

"That's very kind of you, Kate explained. "But we have to catch an eight o'clock plane."

"I'm so sorry," Favier said. "Where else in Europe will enjoy the pleasure of your company?"

"We fly to Munich," Kate answered. "We spend a day or so there and then we cruise down the Danube to Vienna, then a train to Florence and Rome, and then over to Athens."

"*Fantastique*," the curator said. "I'm sure you will have a great time. When you are in Munich you will go see the Neuschwanstein castle, *oui*?"

"The Neu-what-stein castle?" Connie asked.

"The Neuschwanstein castle. It's the one built by King Ludwig, you know the crazy one, Mad King Ludwig," he said, circling his index finger around his head. "It's the same castle as for Disneyland, the how do you call it... *ah oui*, the Sleeping

44

Beauty's castle. It is based on Neuschwanstein. You must go. Anyway, we will see you in November, no? You will come back for the unveiling, as our guest of course? *Oui, D'accord. Bon voyages, mademoiselles. Bon voyages.*"

. . . .

Ten

"I'm sorry," the cab driver told the two American women in the back of his taxicab as he moved the car across the autobahn's traffic lanes positioning himself for the next exit. "On the radio they have just said Neuschwanstein is closed today," he explained in his German accent. "Some water pipes burst. I will come off from the autobahn on the next place and you can decide what to do. Is that okay?"

"That's fine, thank you," Kate McBride said. Then, turning to Connie she said, "There must be something else," and reached into her bag and pulled out a guidebook.

The black Mercedes eased off the highway and the driver brought it to a stop alongside the road, the diesel engine chugging along in a quiet hum.

"Let's see," Kate said thoughtfully thumbing through the book. "Oh, here's something. No, never mind."

"What?" Connie asked.

"You won't want to go."

"Where?"

"Dachau," she told her friend. "That's near here, isn't it?" Kate asked the driver, who pointed to a road sign in front of them and said, "It's just thirty kilometers, maybe fifteen minutes."

"Dachau? What's that?" Connie asked.

46

"It's a city, but it's also the name of one of those concentration camps. You know, from World War Two. There's a museum and a memorial there now. We don't have to go, never mind."

"One of those Nazi camps?"

"Mrs. Klein said she was there."

"Who?"

"Mrs. Klein. You know her, she comes into the shop on Friday mornings just as you're leaving."

"Oh, sure, I know who you mean. She was in one of those?" Connie Perez asked.

"This one."

"That must've been horrible. Can you imagine?"

"No, I can't. That's why I want to go. Would you mind too terribly?" Kate asked the driver.

"Not at all. I understand completely," the man said humbly. "It is important. Everyone should go there at least once so none of us forget."

"I know it's not quite what you had in mind..." Kate McBride told her friend.

"That's okay. Let's go. I *want* to go," Connie affirmed.

Kate McBride paid the cabbie as she and Connie got out and stood there for a moment, staring. When the taxi pulled away a few moments later it startled them. They looked at each other, took a deep breath, and began walking to the camp.

At the entrance, a pair of large, clean-scrubbed, coal black wrought iron gates under a brick portal. Welded into the gates, in a square cut out at the middle, the words "*Arbeit Macht Frei*" greeted them. "Work makes you free," Kate said quietly, reading from her guidebook as they walked through.

"It didn't, though, did it?" Connie asked with a sigh.

"No," Kate said in a low voice as they passed into the camp, a chill running down her spine.

In the building where inmates once turned out two-pound loaves of bread—each one, by the Nazis reckoning they learned, a full day's rations for 16 people—was instead, now a museum. But, Kate thought, museum is the wrong word for this. These exhibits were unlike any she'd ever seen or imagined. There is no science or art here; only the stark realities of human suffering and death.

They pair grew quieter still as the exhibition's somber tones began to wash over them like a rising tide, slowly and hesitantly at first, then faster and with a harsh, cold, frightening certainty.

First came the history lessons, the grainy, life-sized, black-and-white photos depicting Jewish life across Europe before the war: From the centuries-old synagogues and prominent commercial houses in Europe's biggest cities to its poorest roots in the *shtetls,* the small, rural enclaves where Eastern Europe's Jews had retreated over the centuries to minimize the opportunities for persecution. Then came the modern history, the progression of events leading up to the war. Hitler's rise, and the world's reaction: silence followed by appeasement and compromise with the dictator followed soon after by horrific warfare on a scale never before witnessed in history. Then came the geography lessons, the maps

48

and cold, hard statistics: three million Jews plucked from Poland; half a million from Germany; so many hundreds of thousands more from France, and Austria, Hungary and Italy, from the whole of Europe, until the final tally had been tabulated. Out of six and a half million Jews in Europe before the war, nearly all—six million of them—had been annihilated, Kate McBride read silently in disbelief, repeating the number over and over in her mind. Six million. Six. Million. People. Gone. In a world gone mad. How else to account for it, she asked herself, except sheer madness.

Then finally came the pictures, the haunting black-and-white images of otherwise unimaginable cruelty captured in a kind of mute testimony. On these faces, in these gaunt eyes, Kate McBride noticed, there were only two types of expressions: the eerie desperation of those who still held out hope and the eerier-still, unmistakable void of those who had already slipped into hopelessness.

"I'm beginning to understand why Mrs. Klein is the way she is," Kate whispered to Connie. "She's such a nice lady, but in the end, she somehow always seems disconnected from the rest of us, like there was a ghost over her shoulder. There must be a thousand ghosts. A thousand, thousand ghosts."

"Jesus, Mary, and Joseph," Connie said in hushed tones as she stared at the stark images and made the sign of the cross. "God rest their souls."

The women left the building in silence and stepping back out into the glaring sunlight, they stopped and stared out at the courtyard. Where there were once thirty-four ramshackle barracks teeming with the day's condemned, dying, and dead, now there was instead two neat rows of gravel-filled planter boxes, six inches tall, each the length and width of a building, seventeen on one side of the yard, seventeen more on the other, like so many perfectly groomed garden plots.

Surrounding the perimeter of the yard, columns of tall, straight trees stood guard like giant wooden soldiers, casting their long shadows into the courtyard where columns of prisoners once stood. "This is where they did roll call," Kate murmured. "Sometimes for ten, twelve, eighteen hours straight, all night, even in the dead of winter in those paper-thin uniforms we saw inside."

Just outside the camp's machine gun-turreted towers, Kate read, the only building from which no prisoner ever escaped: the crematorium, the sky above it today as blue as it was once was red, its lurid glow lighting up the night sky day after day.

Where once there was only the silence of the living at Dachau, Kate could only hear the enduring silence of the dead now. And inside her silence, like for every other visitor, came the torrent of questions: Why? How could this happen? How could anyone be so cruel? What if it were me?

They walked across the courtyard and sat down along the edge of one of the planter-box barracks, looking out at the pristine emptiness of it all, soaking it in, and then, like others around them, did the only thing they could do faced with the evidence of so many people having been so horribly brutalized: They wept until they could weep no more.

After a time, Connie Perez said, "I don't know about you, but I got chills that won't quit and I can't stop shaking. Are you ready to go?" she sniffled, drying her tears and wiping her nose.

"Sure," Kate answered grimly, pulling herself together, "Sure." She stood up and reached into her bag. "Damn," she muttered under her breath. "I need to go back inside for just a second. I think my lipstick fell out again. I heard something fall when we first started out."

"I'll be waiting out front, I'll get us a cab."

Kate McBride walked across the yard, back into the museum, and scanned the floor, exhibit by exhibit, until she saw the chrome-capped cosmetic glittering beneath one of the black-and-white enlargements, a family portrait.

She reached down and scooped up the lipstick, then paused to glance at the photo one more time. 'Jewish family life, Radom, Poland, circa 1920,' the small caption card read in five languages. At the center of the scene, the papa—a dashing man with a strong, high forehead and a pair of warm, sparkling black eyes—sat stiff and upright in his suit and tie in a high, winged back chair. Seated on a stool beside him, his beautiful bride, one child cradled in her arms, two more holding on fast at her knees, and a fourth just beginning to make itself evident in the woman's profile.

The woman looked to Kate to be ten years younger at least than the man at her side. But unlike most of the other pictures Kate had seen of women from that era, something in this one's demeanor conveyed the message that she was quite content in her life. She had soft eyes, blue or perhaps light gray, and on closer examination, her two eldest children—a blonde, curly-haired pixie three years old at most, decked out in a white sailor's cap and dress, and her younger brother, a curly-haired moppet with his mother's strong cheekbones and his father's plump eyes—seemed not so much to cling to their mother as they did gently cleave to her the way foals do with their mares.

As she turned away and started back outside, something pulled Kate McBride back to look at the photo one more time. Then, in an instant, it became clear. "Sweet...Jesus," she whispered, the blood draining from her face, her hands trembling. There, plain as the contentment on the young mother's face, on the wall behind this long-since obliterated idyllic vision of family life, hanging in a gilded frame above the plush, overstuffed sofa, was the Girl with Flowers. And there, too, Kate could see now, was the very girl herself, a woman—with children cleaving to and her man at her side—but it was her, those eyes still every bit as alive.

The curator's office was small, plain to say the least, understated at best, a model of German efficiency. But although sparse, Kate McBride had to admit, it was suited well-enough for what few tasks it had—overseeing some light grounds-keeping and maintenance, a modicum of record-keeping, and answering the occasional correspondence from those ever-fewer souls looking for a long-lost relative or someone who, while trying to answer a question on a medical history chart, discovered a long-forgotten branch of their family tree.

Seated next to her, Connie Perez reached over to take Kate's hands in hers to comfort her, but Kate pulled back. "Don't," she said nervously. "I'm all sweaty."

"It's going to be alright. Here," Connie said, handing Kate a few tissues from her purse. They sat in a pair of identical stiff, high-back wooden chairs across the desk from the curator, a slight, rumpled man in his late sixties with warm brown eyes and thin, rimless glasses pressed against thick, white eyebrows. Prof. Dr. Hans Bickel, the small nameplate on his desk read.

"This is quite remarkable," the old man said, his voice crackling a little. "I mean, of course I believe you, *fraulein*, but it is such a fantastic story. Simply amazing. Now," Bickel said leaning across his desk, "I am not trying to, how do you say it, give you the brush-off, but it will take some time, maybe a few hours if we are lucky, perhaps a day or so if we are not so fortunate in our searching. May I suggest you continue on your journey and if you provide me your contact information, I will be in touch immediately when—"

"Continue on?" Kate asked incredulously. "I can't continue on. There is nowhere to continue on to until I find out who this family is and whether or not any of them are still alive. No, I can not continue on," Kate McBride said firmly. "I'm sorry," she said in an apologetic tone. "I'm very upset. I knew from the beginning something like this would happen sooner or later. I can't go on. I just can't," she said, starting to cry.

"No, of course not," the curator said. "It is I who should apologize, for suggesting such a thing. You have every right to be upset. Please accept my apology."

"It's not your fault," Kate said sniffling.

"Just please, Fraulein McBride, do not get your hopes up too high, these records can be quite sparse at times," Hans Bickel said shaking his small, gray head and heaving a tiny sigh. "But, may I suggest this, please, *frauleins*? Let me arrange a room for you in town and here is my mobile telephone," he said, handing the phone across the desk to her. "We will begin searching at once and the minute we find something one way or another, I'll call you and send a car to pick you up. I promise. To go through all the possibilities we have should not take more than forty-eight hours. How is that?"

"That's fine," Kate McBride said, drying her tears. "But we can't take your phone. We'll be at the hotel. Thank you. I'm sorry, I just can't believe this is happening. I can't believe it," she said as Connie guided her out by the shoulders.

The suite Hans Bickel had arranged at the Dachauer Inn was nicely appointed in a traditional Bavarian motif, a perfect match for the picture-postcard view of the lush, green German countryside from its flower-filled balcony. Kate paced back and forth as Connie Perez fidgeted on the plush, old-fashioned sofa, clicking through one German language channel after another on the television.

"You're wearing a path in these nice people's rug," Connie said with a smile. "Look, it's gonna be okay. Even if they find something out, and you find a survivor, you did everything you could. They're going to understand."

"Look at all the money I've already spent," Kate said, frantically pulling store receipts out of her purse, flinging them in the air and letting them fall like ticker tape all around her. "There's no way I'll ever be able to pay this back. No way."

"I'm sure whoever painting it is will just be thrilled to get it back and they're not going to worry about a few thousand dollars out of fifty million."

"A few? I've already spent like twenty-five thousand dollars!"

When the phone chirped a moment later, Kate McBride jumped in a fright. Her heart pounding, she scrambled to answer it. "Hello? Hello?"

"*Fraulein* McBride?" Hans Bickel inquired through the phone. "I have some good news. Maybe not everything you want, but a start, a very good start. The car will be downstairs in five minutes."

"We have some details, not everything, but better than nothing," the curator said with encouragement. He slid an eight-by-ten print of the black-and-white photo and some papers out of a large brown envelope and set them down on the desk in front of Kate and Connie.

"This is the Stern family," Bickel explained as he pointed them out in the picture. The papa," he began, pointing a crooked old finger at the dashing young father, "was Josef Stern. And this," he said, softly rubbing his hand across the picture, "this is *the* girl in Girl with Flowers, Hannah Kessler Stern. We don't know the children's names, I'm afraid."

"Hannah Kessler Stern," Kate repeated softly, reaching out and gently taking the picture from the old man. She stared at it and lightly brushed her fingers across Hannah's face.

"Apparently, they ran an insurance business, rather prominent by all accounts, perhaps the largest in Poland, Kessler Insurance," Hans Bickel explained, looking at the papers. "The records show the Sterns were one of the first to be put in the ghetto in early September 1939, about a week after the Nazis invaded Poland on 1 September. Like all the other families, from there they were separated and dispersed to the camps shortly after.

"We have one account saying Hannah Stern was sent to Bergen-Belsen in 1942, and another claiming she was arrested in Budapest in 1944. Either way, it is all we know. Here," Hans Bickel said, gathering up the papers and the photo and sliding them into the brown paper envelope which he pushed across the desk to Kate. "I had photocopies of everything made for you. You can also check the organizations listed here for more information," he added, handing her a sheet of paper.

"Remember," Hans Bickel said fixing his gaze on Kate. "If you find *Frau* Stern, it is difficult to know what to expect," he said in a somber tone. "She will be quite old, as you might imagine. She may not want to talk about her experiences here. This painting may bring back horrible memories or she may have blotted them out altogether. The survivors lead lives that are broken in two: Before Hitler and After Hitler. Not all of them were able to bridge the two worlds successfully. It's not an easy transition," he finished shaking his head back and forth slowly. "If there is anything else we can do, *Fraulein* McBride, please let us know. Please," he emphasized, taking her hand and patting it gently. "Best of luck."

In the car on the way back to the inn, Kate McBride glanced emptily down at the sheet of paper. Addresses and telephone numbers typed in neat little blocks: The Holocaust Museum, Washington, D.C.; The Simon Wiesenthal Center, Los Angeles, California; the Historical Records Archive of the Republic of Germany, Berlin; the Ellis Island Foundation in New York; the immigration departments for the U.S., Canada, Australia, and Britain.

Across the skies over Western Europe and the whole Atlantic Ocean, as they flew home, Kate McBride stared at the names over and over again and wondered which, if any, would tell her if Hannah Kessler Stern or any of her children or grandchildren were still alive. Kate pulled out the copy of the black and white print Hans Bickel had given her and compared it to the picture of the painting from the auction catalog. Hang in there, Hannah, Kate thought. If you're out there, I'm going to find you. I swear I will, she vowed to the Girl with Flowers.

. . . .

Eleven

In the early dawn, Salvatore DeCicco's portly physique cast an equally stout silhouette onto the wall of the brick oven. Kate watched him through the window as he pounded the dough, back and forth, kicking up clouds of flour dust. As he turned to grab his bread paddle, the baker caught sight of Kate in the window and his eyes lit up.

"*Bambina,*" Kate watched him mouth through the glass with a big smile. He opened the door and pulled her in for a bear hug sending up a cloud of white flour dust into the air around them. "Mama, come see, quick," he shouted.

"What? What's all the fuss?" Maria DeCicco asked, pushing open the swinging door from the front of the shop. "Katalina," she shouted as soon as she saw Kate. Then waddling up to her, she hugged Kate with every ounce of her porky, five-foot frame.

"Welcome home, *bambina.* My how time flies. It's been a month already? Papa, why didn't you tell me Katalina was coming home today?" she fussed, shuffling back and forth and pinning the loose strands of her long, gray-black hair back in a bun. "You didn't make a cake, nothing."

"Mrs. D.," Kate interrupted. "It hasn't been a month."

"Of course it hasn't," Sal DeCicco said knowingly, even though he had no idea how long it had actually been.

"I had to cut the trip short. Something came up."

58

"Whatsa matter?" Sal DeCicco asked, a look of concern dissolving away his grin. "You okay? Somebody sick? You friend, Connie, she's okay?"

When she finished explaining the events of the past few days Salvatore DeCicco didn't say a word, he just plucked her old apron from the hook where it had been hanging since she left and handed it to Maria who tied it around Kate's waist and pushed her out to the front of the small shop.

"Good night," Kate said, ushering the last customer out of the store and locking the front door behind them. She snapped the cord down and turned off HOT/FRESH, and watched through the glass as dusk descended on Flatbush like a dark blanket. Then Kate McBride pulled the shades down. "Whew," she sighed, exhausted from a busy day full of explanations to all the regulars who stopped in for a loaf of bread or a dessert cake or half a dozen muffins. As she reached for the stool to begin balancing the till, the phone rang, startling her, and setting her heart racing on adrenalin. "DeCicco's," she answered. "Yes, this is she. I'm Kathleen McBride." She listened and nodded, then quietly said, "Thank you," she said languidly and hung up.

Maria DeCicco stood in the doorway between the back of the bakery and the front, Salvatore right behind her watching her expression for a sign.

"Australian Consulate," Kate explained in a low tone. "No record."

"It's gonna be alright," Salvatore said, gently pushing Maria toward Kate. "Somebody's gonna have a gooda news."

Kate switched off the lights in the glass cases one by one, stopping to scoop up a few crumbs with her hands and dropped them into the trash. She moved toward the back of the shop when there was a knock on the door. "Please," Kate moaned under breath, then in a loud voice, "We're closed."

But the knocking, though light, was persistent. Kate walked over and pulled back the shade, "We're closed. Oh, Mrs. Klein, it's you. Hi," she said, a smile forming on her face. "Just a minute," Kate said, holding up one finger. She reached into her apron, pulled out the key and slipped it into the lock, and then opened the door to let the old woman in. "I was wondering what happened to you this morning. Is everything okay?"

"I'm sorry, I'm sorry," the woman apologized in her thick, eastern European accent. "Tank you. No, everyting is fine. My Martin forgot he had a doctor's appointment, notting serious. Den ven ve got dere de doctor vas late. First ten minutes, den twenty, den an hour and twenty. Until I forgot and it's almost time for supper and I don't have bread for de *Shabbas* table," she said fussing in her purse.

By the time Ruth Klein finished explaining, Kate had her loaf of challah bread wrapped, bagged, and ready to go. She passed the loaf around the side of the counter in the exchange for the crumbled bills the woman extracted from her change purse.

"Wait a minute," the old woman said vaguely. "Am I losing my mind altogether? Didn't you quit? You had de painting and de money and…"

60

"No, you're not losing your mind," she told Ruth Klein with a warm smile and a brief explanation of the recent turn of events. "You tried mit immigration here and in Kenedah? Australia? Israel and Germany?" she asked in her thick accent as Kate nodded yes to each query.

"You tried de Wiesental Center in Los Angelus?" Ruth Klein asked and again, Kate nodded. "And de Hyess?"

Kate nodded again and then stopped. "The what? Hye..."

"Hyess. Aitch, eye, aye, ess," Ruth Klein said spelling it out. "De Hebrew Immigrant Aid Society."

"What's that?"

"Nobody told you from de H.I.A.S.? Dey help people, Jews, to immigrate from countries vere dey are not so welcome to places vere dey are. To America. Israel. Dey help mit de paperverk, de guarantees to de government dat you von't be a burden to dem. Dis H.I.A.S. is around long before de var, over a hundred years."

"What happened to it?"

"Vat do you mean vat happened? Notting happened. It's still dere. Dey have an office downtown on Sevent Evenue."

. . . .

Twelve

"**In June, 1945, the Joint Distribution Committee**, run by the Americans and the British, designated Europe's remaining 500,000 Jews as D.P.s," the clerk at the H.I.A.S. office explained to Kate McBride from behind the counter.

"D.P.s?" Kate repeated.

"Displaced persons. Here we go," the clerk said, scrolling through the screens on her computer monitor, pointing and clicking through the records. "I've got a Hannah Lillian Kessler. Admitted, Port of New York, June 3, 1949."

"That's it, that's her," Kate said, smiling broadly. "Hannah Kessler. This is her in 1917," Kate beamed, showing the clerk the copy of the black and white photograph. "Thank God. Can you write down the address for me?"

"Address?"

"Where I can find her," Kate said, barely able to contain her enthusiasm.

"We just have historical records, Ms. McBride. We don't know where she lives now. Or even if she's still alive."

"How do I find her then? Did she list where she was staying when she got here? Did she have any family here?" Kate anxiously wanted to know.

"I'll print you a hard copy of her landing card," the clerk offered. "Chances are she would have had contact with at least one of the government agencies after she arrived. She would have gotten a Social Security number, driver's license, paid taxes, something. I would start with S.S.A. first. If she is alive, she would be collecting social security or disability and they might have a current address."

"How old do you think would she be now?" Kate wondered out loud as she and Connie Perez navigated their way through the diverse crowd of dependents that inhabited the Social Security office on any given day. She pulled a number from the ticket machine and they walked to the back of the drab room and took up residence in a pair of wobbly, faded-mauve, plastic chairs with a clear view of the digital display that flashed big red numbers at the snail's pace only a bureaucracy this large could produce.

"She'd have to be like, a hundred and ten or something," Connie Perez calculated. "Getting up there. That is, if she hasn't already gone up there," she said, pointing one of her long, glittery fingernails upward.

"She might have children. Grandchildren."

"Even they would be like eighty or ninety. What's our number?" Connie asked.

Kate held up the pink ticket, the number 307 printed in block letters on both sides.

"See that guy over there?" Connie said, nodding toward an especially old, wrinkled pensioner. "He was our age when he came in and he's holding number three."

"Oh he is not," Kate chided with a smile. "Look, they're already up to two-ninety-two and it's moving pretty fast."

When 307 flashed on the screen Kate said, "Let's go," and they walked up to the window where Kate pleaded her case.

"I understand," the woman behind the wired-glass window said sympathetically. "But I can't release any information. The records are confidential, you know that."

"Of course she knows it," Connie answered testily. "We all know it, but what is she supposed to do? If this were your mother or grandmother wouldn't you want them to know they had fifty million dollars? Look, you know and I know she could pay some guy fifty bucks who's just going to go online and come up with the information anyway."

The woman stared at the two of them for a moment. "Oh, what the hell," she finally said, conceding the reality of privacy and confidentiality since the dawn of the internet. "If it is her, maybe she'll stop collecting S.S.A. and there'll be a little extra for the rest of them what needs it more."

"Now, you're talking,' Connie said with an audacious smile.

The woman looked at the paper Kate had handed her and typed in the name. "System's really slow today," she said tapping her nails against the keyboard while they waited. "Bingo. I've got a Hannah Lillian Stern, maiden name Kessler. She's been getting checks since 1982. Here's the address where we're sending them," the woman behind the glass said, writing it down on a piece of scrap paper. "1135 New Jersey Avenue, Brooklyn. And this," she said, writing something else down, was her former employer, Beltsman Manufacturing. Good luck."

. . . .

Thirteen

Moving through the pale afternoon light in her apartment, Kate McBride practiced in the hallway mirror as she tucked her scarf inside her overcoat. "How do you do, Mrs. Stern? Mrs. Stern, I'm sorry," she tried, then started again. "You don't know me. My name is Kate—oh never mind," she conceded, grabbing her purse and running out the door and into the cab where Connie Perez was waiting in front of her building.

"What's with the long face?" Connie wanted to know. "Isn't this is what you've been hoping for all along? The opportunity to give away all that money?"

Kate McBride stared hard at her friend.

"I'm sorry. What's wrong?"

"I'm nervous. What if she's upset?"

"Upset about what?"

"I don't know, just upset."

"Upset that you found her painting and then did everything possible to find her? Upset that you're doing the right thing and turning over fifty million dollars?"

"Not quite fifty million," Kate reminded her. "What if the painting brings up bad memories?"

"That painting? That girl is in love, you can see that in her eyes, the moment you look at her. And it's not just any love, we're talking head-over-heels, can't-remember-what-day-of-the-week-it-is, love."

66

The building at 1135 New Jersey Avenue was a squat, brick box two stories high and a block wide. Two rows of dingy windows spread out across the face of it, each of them trapped behind a rusty layer of wire mesh that made the building look as much like a prison as an apartment, but as she approached the front door with Connie, Kate soon realized it was a nursing home. "Brooklyn Home for the Aging," a tarnished old sign pinned to the bricks outside the front entrance read.

Kate pushed open the front door, and she and Connie Perez walked into the lobby. The yellowed, mildewy walls and the smell of old age—that unmistakable scent of skin ripe beyond its years filled her nostrils—and instantly brought back memories of her own grandmother's last few years. The endless stream of Saturday afternoons dragged to the home in Rockaway, in a dress starched as stiff as a priest's collar, until one day her mother said there would be no more visits to Nana save the one final one, the following Sunday morning at church.

Kate McBride's eyes drifted across the room at the sea of wheelchairs and walkers, the tufts of white hair in wiry clumps and the thin, brittle bones stretching skin whose elasticity had long ago evaporated. Faded, tropical-flowered housecoats outnumbered frayed terrycloth robes by about four to one, she observed.

"Crystal," a woman said, tugging at Kate's arm from behind. "Your mother's been worried about you."

"I'm sorry," Kate answered, taking her arm back gently. "I'll go apologize to her."

"Can I help you?" a short, middle-aged woman asked Kate in a clipped Philippine accent.

"I'm trying to locate a Mrs. Hannah Stern. Is she here?"

"Yes."

"May I speak with her?"

"Why you want to speak to her?" the woman chirped. "Nobody come to see Missy in twenty years."

"I only found out she was here yesterday. May I see her, please? It's very important."

"Who are you? Are you family?"

"No, but if no one's been to see her in twenty years," Connie chimed in, "she may be the closest thing to family she has right now."

"Okay," the nurse relented all too easily, then pointed at a lone figure seated in a wheelchair in the far corner of the day room. "But just you," she said looking at Kate. "You wait outside," she told Connie abruptly.

"No problem," Connie told the nurse, then turned to her friend and said, "I'll be right here if you need anything, sweetie."

Kate didn't say anything then looked across at the small figure on the far side of the room and then back at Connie.

"You'll be fine," Connie reassured her, and when Kate acknowledged with a small nod of her head that she would indeed be all right, Connie turned and headed for the small sofa near the door.

"Thank you," Kate said to the nurse as she walked back to her small desk.

"I'll be watching you," she said without looking back.

Kate took a deep breath and started across the room. As she did, it felt like every pair of eyes in the room followed her every move. As she approached each of them, she watched as a look of hope and anticipation crossed their tired old faces, that perhaps someone were coming to pay attention to them. But then as soon as she passed them, the look would leave every bit as quickly and the sallow pallor of despair would flood back in and restore itself around their hollow cheeks and empty eyes. Kate stopped a few feet behind Hannah Stern and took a moment to compose herself. "Mrs. Stern?" she barely whispered. Then, after clearing her throat, a little more loudly, "Mrs. Stern? Ma'am?"

She walked around to see the old woman's face and was instantly drawn to it. There they were, those same cornflower blue eyes that had taken her breath away the first time she saw them glittering in the moonlight shining down from her mother's attic. That same slight, encouraging smile curled up at the corners of her lips. Her hair, white as a winter bunny now, was still thick and shiny and pulled into a tight bun at the back of her head. A small strand of pearls lay loosely around Hannah Stern's hollow collarbone but her hands were free of any jewelry or polish and they hung limply on the armrests as she sat in her wheelchair, somewhat dwarfed by it.

"Mrs. Stern...you don't know me. My name is Kathleen McBride. Kate."

The woman, her eyes blinking once, nodded slightly.

"I don't know where to begin," Kate said nervously. "I guess I'll start at the beginning. I found this," she said, unrolling one of the prints that had been made from Girl with Flowers. "I

69

mean, I found the original. Rolled up inside a book in my mother's attic. Do you remember this painting from Mr. Chagall?"

Again, the tired, wrinkled eyelids clipped shut for a moment and Hannah Stern nodded ever so slightly.

"I took it to the museum, of Modern Art, and they told me how important a painting it was," Kate McBride continued. "They tried to find you, I tried to find you, but back then we only had the painting to go on. We didn't have your name. We placed ads, did searches, all over the world. Anyway, when no one claimed the painting, I sold it at auction. I mean what was I going to with it? The Louvre, in Paris, bought it. For fifty million dollars."

Hannah Stern's pale, droopy cheek twitched slightly, and again, another, knowing blink of those radiant eyes in the rays of sunlight spilling in through the window.

"Well, I used some of the money, to go on a trip," Kate McBride explained apologetically as she took the old woman's hand. "To Europe. When I stopped at the museum in Dachau, there, on the wall," she said taking the black and white print out of her purse and slipping it into the old woman's hand, "I saw this. Do you remember this picture? Did you know it was at the museum?"

Hannah Stern gave Kate's hand a weak squeeze.

"Well, I felt awful and excited and scared and sad all at once. I knew I had to find you or your family. That was last August. Between the agencies and the government and all it took until now... I guess what I'm trying to say is, I found you now and I want to give you your money, what's left, I mean. I'll pay you back what I've already spent. I don't how, but I will. The money, the fifty million, well, twenty-two million after the fees and taxes, it's yours. Do you have a bank account I can deposit it in for you?"

Having gotten it all off her chest, Kate McBride heaved a sigh of relief.

The old woman lifted her head a notch, looked up at Kate, and parted her parched lips. In a weak voice Hannah Stern said, "You keep it dear."

"Ex...cuse me?" Kate asked, stunned.

"You keep it dear," Hannah Stern repeated softly.

"I'm sorry. Maybe you didn't understand correctly. I found your painting. It sold for fifty million dollars and... the money is yours."

"You keep it dear," the small voice chirped again. And then Hannah Stern turned her head away as if to end the conversation.

From behind Kate, the Filipino nurse interrupted in her clipped accent. "That's all Missy say for twenty years. You want dinner, Missy Stern? 'You keep it dear.' You got to go peepee? 'You keep it dear.' The Martians just landed in Manhattan, John Travolta wants to do nookie-nookie with you," she giggled mockingly. "No matter what you say, Missy say, 'You keep it.'"

"Yes, but she heard what I said. She understood, she nodded," Kate told her.

"Muscle spasms," the nurse said.

"But she squeezed my hand."

"A twitch," the Filipina explained, then added smartly, "Hope what you want to tell her not too important," then walked away.

71

"That's it?" Connie Perez asked as they walked along New Jersey Avenue in the cold, late-afternoon chill. "'You keep it dear,' What's that supposed to mean? I mean, what do you do now?"

"I don't know," Kate McBride said despondently. "She's got no family, no will. Her social security checks deposit directly to the nursing home. She doesn't even have a bank account."

"Then, I've got another question," Connie said as she stepped off the curb to hail a cab. "What do you think she'd want to do with the money? If she had all her senses, I mean."

"How should I know?"

"Find out."

"And just how do you propose I do that?"

"I don't know, exactly," Connie Perez admitted. "But at least you've got a starting point now. You can work backwards from here and take it as far back as you can go. Maybe something will turn up. Somebody might still be alive who knew her. An old neighbor, an ex-boss. There was one photo, maybe there are more in her room. Letters, diaries. There's got to be immigration records, employment records."

The thought settled in on Kathleen like a summer fog, all at once cool and comforting, and at the same time, chilling and a little bit frightening.

"What?" Connie asked impatiently as a taxi pulled over for them. "You got a better idea?"

"No," Kate McBride admitted weakly.

. . . .

72

Fourteen

The next morning Kate McBride rapped softly on the half-open door marked 214. "Mrs. Stern, may I come in?" She opened the door and looked in on the old woman, sitting across the tiny, dim room like a life-size, crabapple doll, limbs limp, her face wrinkles upon wrinkles, leaving only the eyes to evoke any sense of the spark of life in her.

A mirror, or most of one, hung on the wall above a low, whitewashed chest of drawers, its corners chipped and half its knobs missing, across one wall of the room. A single, cockeyed stalk of a floor lamp leaned between Hannah Stern's chair and the ruffled, half-made bed, and there was a small, spare nightstand against the back wall.

"Do you remember me from yesterday, Kate McBride? I found your mother's painting. This one," she reminded the woman gently and set the small, framed print of the painting she had brought as a present, on the nightstand. "Mrs. Stern, I have to figure out what to do with all this money. *Your* money. I don't know what to do, what to say. So, I came here hoping to find some answers," she said as the old woman listened emptily, that same, slight smile pursed on her lips, those bright blue eyes glimmering in the short shafts of daylight filtering in through the sooty window and the metal grating in front of it.

Kate stared into Hannah Stern's eyes as if, somehow, behind their warm glow, the answer lie, waiting to be unlocked with the magic words, just the right combination of syllables and phrases to set them free.

The bits and pieces on top of the dresser didn't reveal much as Kate looked them over. A hairbrush with white strands of hair curled around some of the bristles; a small ceramic cup; some paper clips; and on one corner of the bureau, in a neat little pile, a stack of papers, all exactly the same size. Statements from the nursing home, each one identical except for the dates: Stern, Hannah Lillian Kessler, Account No. 3326501. Brooklyn Home/Aging, 1135 New Jersey Avenue, No. 214, Brooklyn, NY, 10223. Received: $963.22, Office of the Comptroller of the United States Treasury Social Security Administration. Fees: Private room: $287.09. Meals: $311.25. Assisted care: $302.88. Misc.: $62.00. Total fees: $963.22. Balance due: $0.00. Thank you. Brooklyn Home for the Aging.

"What am I supposed to do?" Kate asked.

"You keep it, dear," Hannah Stern parroted.

"I *can't* keep it," Kate said a little desperately. She knelt down in front of the old woman on the cold tile and took Hannah Stern's frail, liver-spotted hands in hers. "Please. Isn't there something you can tell me? Some sign you can give me?" She waited for a response she knew would never come, then after a minute, Kate McBride stood up and walked back to the bureau, staring at her own reflection in the mirror. Behind her, the image of Hannah Stern rocking slowly back and forth as the last few, warm rays of afternoon light cutting across her wizened face and picking

74

up the silvery glints in those powdery blue fields that were her eyes.

One by one, Kate fidgeted with the objects on top of the dresser as she stared silently into the mirror. The hairbrush, the cracked cup, the paper clips. Then, curling up the edge of the invoice on top of the pile. "Hold on," Kate said picking up the statement. "The billing office," Kate whispered, then turned around, a determined look on her face. "May I take one of these?" she asked Hannah, then folded it into her coat pocket.

"You keep it, dear," came Hannah's stock reply.

"I will, but just for a little bit," Kate McBride said with a warm smile and left.

"Thank you for seeing me," Kate told the nursing home administrator seated across the desk from her, as she explained the situation.

"Well," the woman explained, "I know I'm supposed to say, 'It's against the regulations,' but there cannot be any just reason on God's Earth to deny Mrs. Stern her due. I'm sure the information about her former address is archived somewhere, so if you'll just give me a few minutes."

. . . .

Fifteen

As Kate McBride stepped out of the cab into the heart of Flatbush, she clung to the memo where the woman in the billing office had written down Hannah's old address. The sounds and smells of distant lands, from the Caribbean to the Ukraine, filled the street. Children of all shapes and colors played stoop ball between the passing cars down the street. And on the sidewalks old men and women waddled home laden with small sacks of groceries in each hand or towed them in thin, metal carts behind them. Kate glanced at the note and confirmed the address on the building: 662 Dorsey.

Kate went inside where the smells only grew more intense in the dim hallway. She glanced at the few faded names remaining on the mailboxes: Fuentes, Silber, Moreno. Loscalzo, Murphy, Nedemeyer. She folded the paper, put it in her coat pocket, and made her way up the stairs.

When she reached the third floor landing she stopped and stared at the four cold, brown doors there, each with their peephole staring out at her blankly. She took a deep breath and knocked on the door closest to her, 3A.

After a minute, the door opened and a wall of reggae music spilled out into the hallway, along with a haze of smoke and behind that, a tall, wiry, scruffy-haired teenager with no shirt, an Afro pick stuck in his hair, and a gold ring in his nose.

"I know this may sound a little strange," Kate began, "but I'm trying to see if anyone here remembers a woman who used to live in this building. Right there, actually. In 3B. A Mrs. Hannah Stern. Did you know her or do you know if anyone else who lives here might remember her?"

In the blink of an eye the door slammed shut, the face behind it vanishing in another puff of smoke as though it had never been there.

"I guess not," Kate said to herself quietly and walked over to 3C and knocked on it. She waited then knocked again. As she was about to turn and walk away, an old woman's voice came from behind the door.

"Who is it?"

"Oh, hi," Kate said, a bit startled. "I'm sorry to bother you," she said staring into the peephole. My name is Kate McBride. You don't know me. I'm a friend of an old neighbor of yours, Mrs. Hannah Stern, and I'm wondering if you could help me out," Kate explained.

The sound of locks unlatching led to the door being opened, but only the few inches the small chain on the other side allowed.

"What do you want?" a gray-haired wisp of a woman said through the crack.

"Could we talk?" Kate asked. "Just for a few minutes about Mrs. Stern?"

"Nice-a woman," Bella Rinaldi said in a thick Italian accent. "Lived over there," she said pointing at 3B. "Forty-three years. Sucha nice-a people. Her and husband, what wasa his name? Until he passed. What a nice person. Is she okay?"

"May I come in and ask you a few questions? It's important." With that, the door shut, the chain was pulled free, and the door opened again to let Kate in.

Sitting there in the living room, Kate repeated her tale then finally asked, "Do you know if she had any family? Children, sisters, brothers, in-laws?"

"I always only saw justa the two of them. What *was* his name?" the old woman said searching her memory. "He was a barber, used to cut my Vincenzo's hair ona Sundays after church. When Abe passed, that was his name, Abraham—"

"You mean Josef?" Kate asked.

"I only knew him as Abe. I think his middle name was Josef. Anyway, when he passed she stayed on by herself until the day they moved her to that home. She couldn't take care of herself no more. They just came one day and took her away."

"Who? Who came, how did they know?"

"The city came, welfare, whoever comes when you don't have nobody else. I don't know who exactly."

"But it wasn't family?"

"No."

"Do you think anyone from the barber shop would remember her or them?"

"Shop'sa closed now. Ten years at least."

"What about Mrs. Stern, did she ever talk about anyone from her work at..." Kate pulled the slip of paper from her coat. "Beltsman Manufacturing?"

"No,' Bella Rinaldi said finally. "I'm-a sorry."

"Thank you for trying," Kate said. "Can I ask you one more thing?"

"Sure," the old woman said warmly.

"From what you knew about her, what do *you* think she'd want done with the money?"

"I don't know. Some-athing good, I suppose."

"Did she ever mention any charities or things she supported?"

"Hannah Stern support-a everybody and everything. She wasa a very good person. Very good."

"Well, thank you very much for your time," Kate said, standing up to leave. "If you think of something else, would you call me at this number?" Kate asked, then handed her a piece of paper.

"Sure, sure," Bella Rinaldi said, escorting her to the door.

"Goodbye. And thank you again."

"*Buona fortuna,*" the old woman said shutting her door and making the sign of the cross across her heart and head. "*Buona fortuna.*"

"She says she would like to discuss a former employee, a Mrs. Hannah Stern," Kate watched the receptionist say into the phone. "No, I don't think so. Are you with any agency? Unemployment, workman's comp, an insurance company?"

"No. I'm just a friend of Mrs. Stern's."

"A friend," she parroted. "Okay," the woman said, then hung up and escorted Kate McBride upstairs to the boss's office.

"Kurt Beltsman, how do you do?" the tall, fit man coming out from behind the desk said.

79

Kate hesitated for a moment, then answered, "Kate McBride."

Kurt Beltsman's office, a glass-enclosed perch high above the factory floor gave the executive and his visitors, a birds-eye view of the entire operation: a dozen rows of a dozen women each, all of them hunched over sewing machines. In these places, Kate thought, the work was always the same: long, hot, straining, and, low-paying. Only the breed of the workhorses changed as the direction of the waves the immigrants rode in on shifted from decade to decade. This time, as was the case for some time now, the predominant shade tended toward a dark, peanut-buttery Dominican brown.

When Hannah began here, Kate thought, the color palette must have tended more toward the European shades with the remnants of pale Poles and even whiter Russians. Generations before that it was the olive tones of the Italian peninsula on the heels of her own fair-skinned clan as famine pushed them from the Emerald Isle to America's shores, and even they rode in behind the yellow wake of the Mandarins and the Cantonese.

"Is something wrong?" Beltsman asked.

"No, I'm sorry."

"You were expecting someone older, I know. I'm Kurt Beltsman III. My grandfather founded the business. How can I help you, Ms. McBride?"

"Well, now I'm not so sure you can. I needed some information about a former employee, a Mrs. Hannah Stern, but she would've retired long before your time."

"Our employment records only go back about ten years, I'm afraid. And even that's a few years beyond what the law requires."

"Doesn't matter," Kate said weakly. "The kind of information I'm looking for wouldn't be in your files. I was hoping to speak with someone... who might have worked with Mrs. Stern, who might be able to tell me a little bit about her. Well," Kate said, getting ready to leave, "there's no point in taking up any more of your time."

"Oh?" Kurt Beltsman said.

"Thank you very much for seeing me."

"But there is someone," the man said. "Someone who knew her, that is. My grandfather is just down the hall. He may have retired some time ago, but the day he doesn't come into the factory is the day I worry. Let me get him for you."

The elder Beltsman more closely resembled what Kate had envisioned with his thick shock of silvery hair. But he struck her more so for his smooth, tight skin, the clarity and brightness of his slate-gray eyes, and his spry youthfulness, especially when compared to his contemporary, the wisp of a woman whose fate brought her to see him today.

"Good afternoon, I'm Kurt Beltsman," the man said with all the elegance and grace of an ambassador, only the slightest trace of an accent in his smooth voice. "How can I help you, Miss McBride?'

"Do you remember a Mrs. Hannah Stern, someone who used to work for you?"

"Yes, of course I remember Hannah," he said, a broad smile crossing his face. "One of my best employees. A magnificent woman." Then the smile left his face as he asked, "Is she alright?"

"As well as can be expected, I suppose. She's in a home over in Bedford-Stuyvesant."

"She must be getting on. I can imagine," said the man whom the years had treated very kindly indeed.

"I need your help."

"Anything," Kurt Beltsman offered politely. "For Hannah, anything at all."

"Mrs. Stern," Kate began softly as she stared out across the factory floor watching the women work. "Well, she...the thing is, she has no family and it's a little hard to communicate with her because of the Alzheimer's... I guess you could say I'm trying to help put her affairs in order before...you know, before she leaves this world, and if I knew some of the things that were important to her that might be a little easier to do." Kate McBride started to explain the whole story, but then something inside told her not to, so she held her tongue and simply asked, "Can you recall any of the things that were important to her?

"Well," Beltsman said, "that was a long time ago, but let me think about it for a moment. What did Hannah and I ever talk about along those lines? Did we *ever* talk along those lines? That was such a long, long time ago, Miss McBride."

"And I suppose there's no else left," Kate asked, "on the line or in an office, I mean, someone who used to work with her?"

"No, long gone every last one of them. Retired, passed away mostly."

"Well, if you can recall anything at all that might help me..."

"She was a nice girl, worked very hard," Kurt Beltsman began. "Kept to herself as far I was concerned. I know the girls she worked with liked her. They would celebrate birthdays and things together. Little parties, cakes, the usual sort of thing. She was Jewish, I think, no overtime on Friday evenings, that sort of thing. I don't know if any of that helps. As I said, she didn't discuss her private life in any detail. That's the way things were in our day. Not like today, everybody in everybody else's business."

"Do you remember when she began working here?

"In the fifties, sometime. Fifty or fifty-one, probably." A warm smile crossed his face, then he said, "She was such a shy, young girl I almost didn't hire her. I didn't think she could do the work. But she did. And very well, I might add. Never a minute late. Never sick a day. Production like nobody's business. Not like today. The kids today are in, out. They show up, they don't show up. If they're not pregnant, they're—" he cut himself off. "I'm rambling. Sorry. I guess I don't have much to add to your knowledge, Miss McBride. I wish I could've been more help."

"Do you know where she worked before she came here?"

"I think this was her first, and come to think of it, maybe her only, job, in this country. She didn't even speak English when she first started with me, she was fresh off the boat."

"Did she fill out an application?"

"Things weren't quite so formal back then. You hired people based on your gut feeling."

"Any employment records at all?"

"From fifty-three years ago?" he said a little incredulous.

83

"I suppose not. Well, thank you for your time, Mr. Beltsman. I appreciate it."

"I know she may not understand, but please give Hannah my best wishes. Tell her Kurt Beltsman says hello."

"I will," Kate said, starting to leave. "The retirees."

"Excuse me?"

"You said some of the people retired. Do you have any contact information on them?"

"It was such a long time ago. You understand," he said kindly.

"Yes, of course."

That night, a plump, full moon hung outside Mary McBride's attic window as though it were a giant dollop of cream. Sitting motionless on a stack of books, Kate looked out at the bright white sphere. It loomed so large and so close in the clear night sky she remembered back to those lazy, summer nights long ago when she thought she might all but reach out, stick a long, thin straw in it, and suck out its sweet, creamy middle like a thick, vanilla milkshake.

She looked down at the pieces of her life she had assembled around her to try to make sense of it all. "Mama," she told the portrait of Mary McBride she had stood on top of a nearby box, "meet Mrs. Stern." Then, propping up the cover of the auction catalog for her mother to see. "Mrs. Stern, this is my mama."

Call me Mary, she could almost hear her mother say in her soft, warm voice.

And just as warmly, she thought she heard Please, call me Hannah.

"This was Hannah and her family in Poland around 1920 or so," Kate told her mother as she pointed to the copy of the old black-and-white photo the curator had given her. "This is her husband, Josef, and their three children. Hannah lives over in Bedford-Stuyvesant now."

'What a beautiful family,' she knew her mother would say.

She put down the catalog and picked up her mother's picture and set it on the windowsill, the bright moonlight illuminating Mary McBride's face almost as if she were still there.

"What am I supposed to do, Mama?" Kate asked. "I can't keep the money; it's not mine. If I give it to Hannah, it'll only end up going to the government. And like you always said, 'If you're going to do that you might as well just give your money to the circus and get some real entertainment value for it.' I don't even have the authority to use it to move her someplace nicer. And, if I spend it on things for her, like to fix up her room or something, how do I know that's what she'd want done with the money? It's *her* money, I hardly knew how to spend it on myself let alone someone else. What am I supposed to do? Just *what* am I supposed to do now?" she pleaded in a whisper. But this time Mary McBride didn't answer, even in Kate's imagination.

. . . .

Sixteen

"**Hello-o-o?**" **Kate said knocking on the door.** "Mrs. Stern? It's me, Kate McBride. May I come in?" she asked, twisting the knob and entering the tiny room.

Hannah Stern stood and stared out the window into the gray afternoon light, her back toward Kate, her two small, frail hands resting lightly on the dusty windowsill. A dark blue dress with a narrow white lace collar hung loosely around Hannah's limp, petite frame. When she turned around, Kate could see that Hannah Stern had a small, black, woolen scarf drawn around her face, its ends tied clumsily beneath her chin.

"Were you going out? Did I catch you at a bad time?" Kate asked, but the woman just turned back toward the grid of sunlight filtering in through the wire mesh and the sooty, winter-drenched windowpane. "I've been to see some of your friends, Mrs. Stern. I visited with Bella Rinaldi," Kate said, looking for a sign of recognition in the old woman's glassy eyes at the mention of a familiar name, but none came. "Do you remember Bella, from your building? She told me how your husband, Abe, used to cut her husband Vincenzo's hair on Sunday afternoons. Remember?"

Hannah Stern turned back toward Kate, her face half in light, half in shadow. Much like the old woman's life, Kate thought, the life she lived now, her memories locked in darkness, and the one she must have lived before. Slowly, Hannah Stern

87

separated her parched lips. "You keep it dear," the old woman said flatly, then turned her face away yet again.

"Well, anyway," Kate sighed, "Mrs. Rinaldi said to say hello, she sends her best. I also went over to the factory. Beltsman's up in the Bronx. I saw Mr. Beltsman. He says hello too. He remembers you very well, says you were one of his best employees. He was nice. They both were, very nice people. But I... I still don't know what you want me to do with your money," she said moving closer to the woman. "And I can't just 'keep it,'" Kate said with a gentle smile. "That's not an option. Can't you give me some kind of sign? *Something*?" she pleaded in a low voice.

The next morning Kate stood across the street from DeCicco's Bakery in the dark, chilly air and watched through the storefront windows as Maria DeCicco got the shop ready. Kate watched as she drew up the shade at the front door quickly, frightened for a moment until she recognized Kate.

"You scare me half-a to death, whatsa matter you, Katalina?" the woman said letting her in. "Since-a when you come ina the front door?"

"Sorry, Mrs. D," Kate answered. "I don't know what I was thinking," she admitted, then grabbed her apron and started setting out the cookies and cakes until they had everything ready to open the shop. When they were done, Kate McBride turned on the HOT/FRESH sign and opened the front door. As she did, Ruth Klein walked in.

"Mrs. Klein, hi," Kate said. "How are you?"

"I've got nothing to complain about," the woman said. And then a beat later, she added in a deadpan, "And if I did, who would listen? Everything is fine, knock wood," she said rapping her knuckles on the side of her head with a smile. "How's by you?"

"I'm okay," Kate said unconvincingly.

"You're okay," Ruth Klein said sarcastically. "And I'm the Queen of England. "Maybe somebody else you can fool, but not me," she said. "What's the matter?"

Kate walked back behind the counter, poured out two cups of coffee and then explained her predicament as the old woman listened intently and then said, "Did you look to see if dere's a society from her town?"

"What do you mean?"

"A society, a club," she explained in her thick accent. "After de var, a lots of us survivors got togeter mit each otter by de towns vhere ve vere born. To find old friends, neighbors. Vee couldn't go back home. Home to vhat? De buildings vas destroyed, de businesses vas destroyed, the synagogues. Everyting. Vhat vas left, dere vas already otter people living dere. So, to keep de memories alive of vhat used to be, to support each otter from who vas left, vee formed societies from the towns vee grew up in. I vas from Nagyvarad, in Hungary, so I belonged to the Nagyvarad Society in New York. Dere vas anotter branch in Montreal and anotter vun in Sydney. Vhere is dis voman from, vhat city?"

"Radom, Poland."

"So look for Radom Society, or Radomer Society, maybe somvun is still alive who knows from her."

"Where do I look for something like that?"

"Vhere else?" the old woman asked picking up her package of bread and heading out in the morning light. "Like everyting today, it's on de Internet," she said smiling and walked out the door.

. . . .

Seventeen

What few leaves remained on the trees lining Jerome Avenue in the Bronx were crisp and brittle, and with each gust of wind they clung tenuously to the stark branches. Not unlike the few remaining Holocaust survivors, brittle and clinging to life, Kate McBride thought as she looked down at the scrap of paper on which she'd written down the address for Miriam Reich, recording secretary of the Radomer Mutual Society of New York.

The building at the corner of 164th Street looked tired. Its bricks sagged at the corners and the mortar had receded from between them like the gums of an old dog. Kate scanned the weathered building directory for 4B and finding it, pressed the buzzer. A minute later the door buzzed and she pushed herself through the heavy wood and glass door into the dimly lit hallway.

She threaded her way around the cracked and missing floor tiles and started up the old marble stairway with its smoothed, wooden handrails and rusty, wrought iron pickets. By the third landing Kate began to wonder how Miriam Reich did this, even once in a while, let alone everyday. At the fourth floor Kate turned out of the stairwell, into the corridor, and navigated down to the small alcove at the end. As she approached 4B, the door opened, and a voice with only a slight accent said, "Come in, come in. You're Miss McBride, right?"

91

"Call me Kate, please," she said looking at a surprisingly young-looking woman. The years had been much kinder to Miriam Reich than Hannah Stern. Standing in her blouse and slacks, she was trim and fit and her step was still lively. And though she must have been eighty-five, Miriam Reich could have passed for sixty without question.

"Come in," Miriam told her.

A pungent-sweet fragrance wafted out into the hallway from the apartment and an oddly bittersweet music crackled softly on a phonograph from one of the back rooms. Crossing the threshold, Kate felt drawn in, as if to a different world, a different time. "Mmm, that smells delicious," she said.

"*Tzimmes,*" Miriam Reich said. "You know from *tzimmes?*" she asked, though she didn't wait for a reply. "It's a stew, from carrots and raisins."

"Thank you very much for seeing me."

"Why wouldn't I see you? Lilly and I were neighbors back home. We went through the camps together."

"Lilly?" Kate McBride asked nervously, fearing that perhaps the years hadn't been as kind to Miriam Reich mentally as they had been to her physically. "You mean Hannah, don't you?" she corrected gently.

"To the outside world, she was Hannah. To those of us who knew her from back home in Radom, she was Lilly. When they killed Hannah in the ghetto, Lilly took her mother's name. They looked so much alike, no one could tell from the passport. Lilly figured the Nazis wouldn't look for someone who was already dead. She survived that way for a long time. We did anything to survive back then. Some things worked, some didn't."

92

So, the Mrs. Stern I met in the nursing home is not... the same woman as in the painting?"

"No, that's Lilly's mother, Hannah. Hannah is the real Girl with Flowers."

"But the eyes..." Kate said.

"She has her mother's eyes, absolutely," Miriam Reich said smiling warmly.

"When was the last time you saw Mrs. Stern?"

"I don't know, last week Tuesday probably. I stop by every week, usually on Tuesdays."

"But the nurse at the home said—"

"*Oy*, don't start me on the nurses at that place," Miriam Reich interrupted. "I wish I had the money, I would have Lilly stay here with me. But the kind of care she needs the government only pays to institutions. So, I keep in touch. She doesn't say anything, well, you know, you've been with her. But I know she knows I'm there, I can feel it. She knows you're there. She just can't say anything. Who knows why? She was fine for the longest time, but then after she lost her Abie... Anyway, please, sit down," she continued, and led Kate into the living room, itself another step back in time.

A couch once overstuffed and fluffy, now just worn and flabby, filled one wall. Two equally deflated matching chairs with small figurines carved into the gargoylish-looking wooden legs flanked the sofa on either side. And in the corner, the crackling sound of a clarinet wailed quietly on the old phonograph she had heard from the entryway. The end tables separating the furniture were filled with photographs of children and grandchildren, cousins, friends, even an old black-and-white print of Miriam and Lilly in swimsuits at some beach.

"That was the Black Sea," Miriam Reich said picking up the picture. "We spent summers there, Lilly's family, my family, and a few others from the neighborhood. We used to go every summer for two weeks at the end of July. It was a very nice place."

"You know from klezmer?" Miriam turned and asked.

"Pardon me?"

"Klezmer. This music. You know it?" she asked turning up the record player a bit and humming a few notes with the bittersweet music. Miriam Reich walked over to a bookcase in the corner and, moving aside some picture frames, pulled a heavy, gray, canvas-covered volume from the top shelf, then motioned to Kate to join her further back in the tiny apartment. "Come, you'll have some *tzimmes* and I'll tell you about Lilly and Hannah... and of course, Marc and the painting." She moved into the kitchen and spun into motion, stirring pots, tasting and adding dashes of this and dollops of that to the four pots she had going at once on her stove. "And then, maybe afterward, you'll know what to do with the money," she said with a twinkle in her eye.

Kate's heart leapt at the hopefulness those six words— 'what to do with the money'—unleashed.

Miriam Reich raised a hand to wipe the sweat from her brow and there, for the first time, Kate noticed the blue numbers tattooed into the white, fleshy under-part of her forearm more than sixty years earlier; her serial number, as if she were just another semi-durable asset in the grand scheme of Nazi inventory. She imagined she could read the logbook now, 'Item No. D4392, Jew, female.'

For the first time, as if faced with the official Nazi stamp of authenticity, the bone-chilling reality of the Holocaust sank into Kate's mind. Miriam Reich was not some sterile, black-and-white picture, not some history lesson, some statistic, or artifact in a museum. She was the real thing. A survivor.

"*Zetz die anidder*," the old woman said in Yiddish. "Sit yourself down," she translated.

A teakettle began whistling and Kate watched as Miriam Reich shut off the flame beneath it. "Tea?" she asked.

"I'm fine, thank you," Kate said.

"Have tea," Miriam Reich said firmly and poured out two small glasses, handing one to Kate. She sat down at the table in the chair closest to the stove and slowly ran her hands over the cover of the big, gray book she had pulled down from the shelf, her fingers stopping to caress the Polish text embossed on it. "The Book of Radom," she translated. "That was the name of our city. I lived at No. 4 Walowa Street. Lilly and her family lived at No. 12."

Miriam Reich took a deep breath and pried open the cover, flipping past the blank leaves to the cover page and stopping at the black and white photo there. "This was Rynek, the city hall square," she said. "In this building," Miriam Reich showed her, "was my mother's shop. It was a millinery shop, we sold hats. My mother made the most beautiful hats. With feathers and veils. People came from all over the city to buy her hats."

The old woman paused and sipped some tea. "Here. Here was Lilly's grandfather's office," she said, pointing to a large building at the corner of the square. "Kessler Insurance. It was the biggest insurance company for five hundred kilometers at least.

Three stories high, with rows and rows of clerks on every floor. In those days in Poland, that was a very big company. He was a very respected businessman, Jacob Kessler was. Even the Tsar needed Kessler Insurance," she said turning the page. "This is the Vizhnitzer rabbi," she said pointing out the photo of an elderly man dressed in a long black coat and a black hat with a band of fur around the brim. He had a long, white beard, and the side locks worn by ultra-religious Jewish men. "He was the biggest rabbi in all of Poland," she said proudly. "They came from all over for his advice. From Poland, from Belarus, from the Ukraine. He was a very wise man," she said thoughtfully.

"This was the synagogue," she said rubbing her hand slowly over the picture on the following page. "This was our school," Miriam continued, pointing to the picture of high school students cheerfully posed as a class in front of the building. "Our teacher, Mrs. Weingart. Her husband was the milkman. Here. Here's me," Miriam Reich said, pointing a crooked finger and continuing to pore over the young faces frozen in time. "This is my brother, Mayer. My cousin, Sheah. His sister, Leah. Here's Lilly…" she finally said, her voice trailing off. "*Oy*," she sighed, "that was such a long, long time ago. Another lifetime altogether. In fact, for the story of the painting, we have to go back even further, two lifetimes, Lilly's and Hannah's. Hannah was Lilly's mother," she explained.

Miriam Reich took a long, slow sip of tea and closed her eyes as it went down her throat. "Ahh, Hannah," she said with a warm smile. "Hannah was an angel. There's no other way to explain her. When you were in her presence you felt special, you felt alive, connected into the universe like never before. She had such a way about her…

"It began in 1910 before Lilly was born, when her grandfather, Jacob Kessler, insisted Hannah go to Prague to study insurance so she could take over the business one day…"

. . . .

II

Eighteen

Moscow

October 28, 1910

8:00 a.m.

At seventeen, Hannah Kessler had seen that look in her father's eyes a thousand times before. She had seen it with her mother when she was still alive but only rarely. She saw it in business meetings and with insipid salespeople and churlish waiters. She knew that when Jacob Kessler focused his smoldering, raven-black eyes this intensely, when the hairs in his full white beard bristled like they were now, even wild animals knew better than to cross him. Nonetheless, she had to ask one more time.

"Please, Papa. Please," Hannah pleaded as she struggled to keep pace alongside her father as they made their way through the crowded lobby of the central train station. As though he were royalty, the crowd seemed to open up ahead of Jacob letting him through and only closing back again when he and Hannah, and the small tower of luggage being wheeled along in his wake—its struggling porter obscured by the mountain of valises and steamer trunks—had passed as well.

As they passed carts with crates full of honking geese and vendors hawking everything from reading materials to fresh-roasted chestnuts, Hannah Kessler hoped against hope to derail her own locomotive, but Jacob Kessler would brook no such thing. He continued on brusquely passing the urchins singing Russian folk songs for their supper and the tin cups literally being offered up by the blind should a spare kopek or an errant zloty literally drop from the sky.

"Final call, Train No. 52. Warsaw, Prague, Berlin, and points west," the conductor shouted out as the locomotive belted out two steaming blasts of its whistle. "Final call, Number Fifty-two. All aboard."

Without missing a step, Jacob Kessler turned his head and barked back toward the pile of cases and trunks following behind them. "Franz, hurry up!"

Behind the pile of steamer trunks and hatboxes, leather-belted valises, and densely woven carpetbags, a frail, young man struggled to keep up with Jacob. He had thick black hair, cropped close at the sides revealing his two large, pinkish ears and a pair of dark, vacant eyes set deep inside his skull. Combined with his pale, gaunt cheeks he looked as much like a cadaver as he did a living, breathing soul and were it not for just that—his huffy breath condensing in the chill air—the difference between the two at times was barely perceptible.

Hannah skipped a step ahead of her father, this time planting herself squarely in his path, her wavy blonde hair still bouncing, "I don't want to study insurance. I don't want to. I *won't!*" she insisted.

Without a word, Jacob Kessler grabbed hold of his daughter's arms, twisted her around on her heels and, pinching her tightly at the elbows, dragged her toward the train lumbering and hissing just a few yards ahead of them now.

"Papa. Papa," she shouted. "You're hurting me."

At that, Jacob Kessler stopped in an instant, the cart behind crashing into him and the suitcases tumbling down all around them like a pile of children's play blocks. Virtually unaffected, Jacob Kessler released his grip and put his big, beefy hands tenderly on the slender shoulders peeking out from his daughter's shawl. He looked deep into her eyes—those same two cornflower blue fields glistening in the warm, summer sun as her mother's before her and said, "I'm sorry." Then he paused and took a deep breath to compose himself. "We've been over this a hundred times already, Channeleh," he said, using the name he always used when reciting her favorite bedtime stories. "You cannot stay. What will you do here?"

"You know exactly what I will do," Hannah pleaded for the hundredth time.

"This? This is what you want?" he said, pointing at a gnarled, peasant woman clutching a bunch of wilted flowers for sale at the track's edge."

"That's not what I mean and you know it."

"Growing flowers is not a profession."

"It will be the way I'll do it."

"You can not make a living this way. Can *not*," the old man said irrefutably. "No one makes a living from flowers. Who buys flowers except in charity?" he said, taking a coin from his pocket and taking the limp bouquet from the old woman.

"Mama did," Hannah said bluntly.

"You know what I meant. There aren't many people like your mother. Flowers grow on the streets, in the fields. You can spit in any direction and hit a dozen bouquets of flowers free for the taking."

"People will buy my flowers, Papa. They'll be different, better. Their colors will be more vibrant, their fragrance sweeter. I will have a shop in the heart of the city, maybe a dozen shops in all the right neighborhoods, and we will sell nothing but flowers. And they will be arranged in the most beautiful ways for every occasion. Weddings, parties. Mine will be the *best* flowers in the world, Papa," Hannah Kessler said with every ounce of conviction she could muster.

Pulling his daughter closer, Jacob Kessler seemed to waver a little, the blocking in his square shoulders tapering slightly. A slight smile lifted his cheeks. "If you grow them… my Channeleh… I am certain of it." But then, his spine stiffened again and he continued. "Nonetheless, growing flowers is not a job. I'm getting on in years. Insurance is complicated. You will need to understand the business to teach it to your husband and someday, to your children. At the institute, they will teach you. Lord knows, you won't be able to count on this *shlemiel*." He turned back around. "Kafka, you idiot, what in the name of the Almighty are you doing? I swear, when we get back home to Prague, I'll…" he growled under his breath, then lifted the final trunk the slight man had been struggling with back onto the pile as if it were filled with feathers.

"Sorry, sir," Kafka mumbled. Then under his breath he added, "Sorry I ever met a cockroach like you."

Jacob Kessler approached the rail car as he did everything else—as if he owned it.

"Welcome aboard, Mister Kessler," the conductor gushed. "Miss Kessler," he continued, taking the young woman's hand and helping her to board. Hannah turned around and pleaded with her father with her eyes one final time.

"I'm sorry, Channeleh. It's what must be," Jacob Kessler said solemnly, that faint tremor undulating softly in his voice that comes from having to pain your children even when you know it's for their own good.

. . . .

Nineteen

Vitebsk, Russia

October 28, 1910

3:00 p.m.

Under the barren, wintry branches of a large chestnut tree hanging over the frozen waters of the Western Dvina where it intersected with the Vitba and the Luchesa rivers, Moishe Siegel hunched forward, resting his gloved hands on his kneecaps as he squiggled back and forth on his ice skates, huffing and puffing, and trying to catch his breath. Alongside him, his younger brother, Aaron, a full head taller than Moishe, also gasped for air.

"That's three in a row," Moishe said, grinning broadly between gulps for air. "Fifty meters, a hundred meters, and two hundred meters. Face it, Aaron, you'll never beat me. Ever."

The young men swayed back and forth on their skates, their breath floating out in front of them like three-dimensional punctuation marks, capping off each sentence in midair then evaporating into the wind. "Those are only the short distances," Aaron Siegel shot back. "I can take you in the long haul, easy."

Though his brother shivered in a thick wool coat, scarf, hat, and gloves, Moishe seemed fine in just his gray sweater, a pair of suspenders holding up his loose-fitting pants, and the thin, woolen cap pulled over his ears, from which wild snippets of his thick, brown hair peeked out in all directions. His frame was lean and muscular and Moishe Siegel seemed well-suited for this weather. He had a large, sharp nose that defined his face, and thick eyebrows that punctuated his eyes—two grayish-blue pearls with silvery glints that sparkled like tiny diamonds in the late afternoon sun.

To Moishe, Vitebsk in the winter was an ice palace. The pure white snows flown in on fresh Siberian winds wiped the town clean of its bleary squalor and with each crystalline flake that fell from the sky every hovel and shack glistened more and more like a white castle against the big canvas of blue sky. In his mind, in winter, Vitebsk became the fairytale land of his childhood dreams, where big, white stallions pulled sleighs filled with good friends' laughter.

"Not a chance," the cocky young sprinter said still huffing.

"You want to bet?" Aaron Siegel taunted.

The young man stared at his brother, nostrils flaring, the steam roaring out of them like a racehorse. "You're serious? I just beat you three times in a row."

"You want to know how serious I am? You want to go to Paris and study your painting, right?"

"Yes," Moishe huffed into the chill air. "So?"

"And I want to go to Berlin and take my physics studies more seriously. But alone, neither one of us has enough money to go. And the way things are going, we probably never will. But combined, we have enough money for one of us to take a shot at it. So let's make this interesting, shall we? In two hours there's a train passing through Kozyolsk on the way up to Minsk. An hour later the westbound transcontinental comes through headed for Paris and Berlin.

"So, here's what I propose: I'll race you from here to the Kazanskaya Church. The first one to skate past the spires gets the loser's money and... a shot at making their dreams come true. The loser stays here until fortune dictates otherwise. No hard feelings, no jealousies... ever. In less than a week either you'll be in Paris studying under the masters or I will be in Berlin discussing quantum theory with Herr Einstein. What do you say?"

"On your best day I could skate there backwards faster than you," Moishe Siegel bragged.

"Well, if you're so sure, put your money—and your future— where your mouth is," his brother said extending his hand. "I don't know about you, but I'm tired of peeling potatoes and making pickle barrels. I don't want to be a herring monger the rest of my life like Papa."

"You're on," Moishe Siegel finally said, pumping his brother's arm vigorously.

The pair broke loose of each other and Aaron called out to a young girl, ten or eleven years at the most, skating past them. "Hey, Beatrice, come here. We need you to officiate something."

The girl, slid up beside them and Aaron explained the terms of the race. "Moishe and I are going to race to the church and we want you to be the judge of who crosses the finish line first," he told her.

"That's five kilometers from here at least," she whined.

"Precisely," Aaron agreed. "But that's on ice. If you cut across the meadow, you'll be there in no time. Besides, it's on your way home and you know how your mother worries if you're not home by four, it's nearly that time now. "We'll give you a few minutes head start to get there and take a position where you can see the finish line clearly. The outcome could be very close so you have to be able to see exactly who wins."

"I know," Moishe suggested. "Position yourself by that big boulder in front of Reb Frydman's place. If you stand just right, you will have a perfect viewpoint to see who crosses first. When you get there, have him fire off his musket twice. Once to let us know that you've arrived, and a second volley about ten seconds later. That one will be our starting gun. You got it?"

The girl nodded and smiled. "I've got it cousin Aaron, cousin Moishe. One shot when I get there, then ten seconds later another," she confirmed. "First one to cross the spire wins." she said, then turned and ran up the embankment and out of sight.

As he began to carve a pit into the ice with the toe of his skate from which to push off at the start of the race, Moishe asked, "You're sure you want to do this?"

"I'm sure."

"You've haven't beaten me on skates since I was twelve years old. I could win this race with one hand tied behind my back," Moishe Siegel bragged.

"You could… but I don't think you will, big brother. You know why? Because it's a long way from here to the church and you'll have plenty of time to think along the way. And I know you. You'll be thinking that if you win, then you'll actually have to go out and do something. And that thought scares you to death. If you win, you can't just sit here in tiny little Vitebsk and shoot your big mouth off about what a great painter you are. You'd have to do something, *say* something with your art, something important.

And, not only are you afraid to face your fears but worse... you're afraid to face your dreams. What if you fail, you'll ask yourself. Then what? What will people say, if the great Moishe Siegel fell down off his perch once or twice like the rest of us? Anybody between here and St. Petersburg knows you can paint, Moishele," his brother pleaded warmly. "Your landscapes make the hillsides jealous. Your faces practically walk off the canvas. It doesn't take an expert to see that. But lots of others can do that too. Sure, you can make them look with your brushes and your colors and your shadows. But what do they see when they look? Why should the world listen to you, Moishele? And if they do listen, what do you have to say...from here?" Aaron Siegel said, clutching his hand in a fist over his heart.

Moishe's cheeks grew flush as if a floodgate had been opened and he fumed at his brother, his fists clenching open and shut, his legs nervous and jumpy. But then, as the first blast of their neighbor's gun echoed in the crisp air the color left just as quickly, until Moishe Siegel's cheeks were completely drained of their pinkish hue, replaced now instead by the chalky pallor of reality.

His brother looked him squarely in the eye, extended his hand, and said, "No hard feelings, no jealousies. Ever."

"Ever," Moishe Siegel agreed shaking his brother's hand firmly, even as his leg muscles twitched and burned inside his pants as he did.

At that, the second shot rang out and in a burst, the brothers began carving up the ice like lumberjacks with ice picks on their shoes.

By the first turn, Moishe had already moved five meters ahead of his brother with the gap widening, but they both knew that meant nothing. It was only after they reached the long, open stretch between here and the old church, that the true test would come.

By the time he breezed past the last few skaters hanging around in front of the union hall, Moishe Siegel was twenty strides ahead of his brother, but now the gap remained steady and soon, eyeing each other, the pair fell into a steady rhythm, heads down, arms swinging high and fast, and legs pumping out the count—left, right, left, right, one, two, one, two. Down the river, the icicles glistened beneath the crooked branches whizzing by overhead like a million comets in a steady, twinkling stream across the sky.

The skaters pressed on, beads of sweat forming on their brow. Then, just as quickly as they formed, they were brushed back into their windblown hair by the chill winds blowing across their cheeks. By the third kilometer, as they both knew they would, Aaron Seigel's words began to weigh on the young painter. So much so, that by the time Moishe reached the hairpin turn before the final stretch, his lead was reduced to just five strides. Moishe Siegel could almost feel his brother's hot breath panting on the back of his neck.

With five hundred meters to go, the pair were head to head and going all out, the spray of ice from their skates flying up behind them like geysers. As they reached the two hundred meter mark, the skaters put their heads down in a final push to the finish, and when Moishe Siegel screwed himself down for the last fifty meters and crossed the line barely one stride ahead of his brother, his heart was beating so hard he fairly thought it would burst out of his chest.

Aaron Siegel took the results without as much as a wince, even when young Beatrice declared as much out loud over and over again. "Cousin Moishe won, cousin Moishe won."

The men circled the ice for a few moments longer, gasping for air and catching their breath, watching the wisps of smoke curl out of the chimney from the rectory next door to the chapel. Finally, they skated off the ice and sat down underneath a thick, heavy branch hanging down at the river's edge. Moishe broke off a pair of icicles and they each began to suck down its cooling ice.

"Congratulations," Aaron finally said looking his brother straight in the eye and breaking the cold, heavy silence.

"Look, this was stupid," Moishe replied, tilting his gaze down. "Just forget it. Forget the bet, forget the whole thing. Let's get home for *Shabbas* before Mama twists both of our ears off," he said, eyeing the setting sun.

"You won fair and square," Aaron told his brother, reaching out a hand to pull him up."

"I know I did, but come on, be reasonable," he said as they tugged off their skates and replaced them with boots. "And don't start in about me again. What you said was true. I *was* scared. But in the end, I beat you. I could go if I want to, but this isn't the way I want my big break, at my brother's expense."

"That's not it at all. Look, Moisheleh, I meant what I said. If I won I was prepared to leave you behind, no hard feelings. But let's face it," Aaron Siegel said a smile curling up at the edges of his mouth. "When was the last time the Tsar gave a Jew an exit permit to go study at the university in Berlin? That would be...

never. To be a toilet cleaner, perhaps," he laughed, "but not a physics student."

As the boys' small shack came into view on the horizon, Aaron Siegel put his arm around his brother's shoulder and looked him square in the eye. "I'm a decent scientist, but I'm not that good and I never will be. You, on the other hand, have an amazing gift from God himself. It would be a sin to let it stay here in Vitebsk and rot. You'll figure out what to tell the world... and it will listen to you. I am sure of it. And then, I'll be able to say, 'That's my little brother, the famous artist, Moishe Siegel.'"

"All right, I'll go..." he said giving his brother a bear hug. "But Moishe Siegel stays here in Vitebsk. The man getting on the train will be Marc Chagall."

"Excuse me?"

"Don't get upset."

"Who's upset?" Aaron asked unconvincingly.

"For the last five hundred years, all the great painters have come from western Europe. People expect them to be French, or Italian, or Dutch—anything but a Jewish peasant from Vitebsk. Equally important, they expect them to have names that sound like it. Da Vinci, Rembrandt, Monet, Renoir. Look, it's just one less obstacle between the critics and me. Once people have bought my work, and displayed it in their galleries and museums, and made a big fuss over how good it is, it'll be too late for the anti-Semites among them to dismiss it. They'll have already gone on record about the merits of the work and I'll be established."

"Ok then. Just be smart about it." Aaron Siegel cautioned.

"What's that supposed to mean?"

"It means don't tell Mama until after you've sold at least a few paintings, and Papa, well—God forbid it shouldn't happen for a long time—but Papa you shouldn't tell until his gravestone is up and maybe not even then," Aaron laughed. "Come on, let's go. You'll miss your train."

"It's *Shabbas* in twenty minutes, boys. Go wash up," Feige Siegel told her sons as they came through the front door. The tiny woman whirled around the dinner table, dancing around her seven other children, as if she were on roller skates, setting up linens and silverware, as she went.

"Mama, I–" Moishe started.

"Your father will be home any second now and I need you, Moishele, to run over to Reb Mendel's and get another loaf of challah before he closes. And you, Aaron, I need you to get the candelabra down," the woman chattered on. "Your sister is bringing home Shmueley the blacksmith to eat with us tonight and I don't want him to think we can't afford enough bread for a decent *Shabbas* dinner. We can't, but he shouldn't know that. At least not until after she marries him."

"Mama, stop," Moishe said, gently taking his mother's hands. "I need to tell you something."

"After you bring back the *challah*."

"I'll get the *challah*, but listen, please," he pleaded and finally got her attention. "I'm not staying for dinner. In fact... I'm catching a train from Kozyolsk to Paris in about an hour."

"What? Paris? What are you talking about?" Feige Siegel asked, a little confused.

"I've gone as far as I can go in St. Petersburg. They have nothing left to teach me."

"In all of St. Petersburg, they have nothing to teach you? Fine, all right," the woman said. "So you'll go to Moscow. I don't know how but your papa and I will arrange it. We got you the permit to live in St. Petersburg, we'll find a way to get you a permit to live in Moscow."

"I made a bet with Aaron and I won," Moishe Siegel explained.

"Aaron. Since when does Aaron know what he's talking about?" she lamented.

"Listen, Mama. I'm going to get your *challah*. Then I'm coming back, packing a few things, and then, I'm going to Paris." As he watched his mother's expression go from confusion to shock to disbelief, Moishe Siegel explained, how this all came about. "It's something I have to do, and for me, it's now or never."

Feige Siegel's throat grew dry even as her eyes grew wet, then she took her son, by now a head taller than her, by the shoulders. "Well," she began with a stern look. But then she conceded and her attitude softened, "I understand. You have a dream and you have to follow it or you'll spend the rest of your life wondering what would have happened if only you'd done this or that… and I don't want that for you too," she sighed, then kissed him on the forehead. "Go. Your papa will understand. Just not today, so hurry up and leave. I'll explain it to him when it gets home… after he falls asleep at the dinner table," she said smiling, then she hugged her son and sent him packing.

112

Brushes and tubes of paint flew into the battered suitcase on the small bed. They took their places side by side with socks and woolen long johns as Moishe gathered his things.

"Mama, I'm ready," he finally said. "Have you seen my No. 20 Kolinsky? Mama, have you seen my sable brush?" he asked coming around the only corner in the cramped hovel, the one separating the bedroom from the kitchen. As he did, he bumped into his mother carrying two-year-old Tzeitel—the youngest of her brood of nine— the item in question pressed firmly in the teething toddler's drooling mouth.

"Tzeitel," the young man admonished her softly, taking the brush back and wiping the spittle on his trousers. "This is my most expensive one," he chided as he gave her a kiss, then threw the brush into the trunk and shut it.

"So, she has expensive tastes," Feige Siegel said. "You should talk, Mr. Going-to-Paris-Big Shot-Artist."

"Speaking of big shot artists," the slender young man said putting his head down slightly. "I… I'm not Moishe Siegel anymore."

"Who are you, the Tsar?"

"Please, Mama. In the eyes of the world, someone named Moishe Siegel is a Jewish peasant from Vitebsk," he explained, taking his mother's worn hands in his palms. "The only thing people want to buy from a Moishe is a tailored suit. Art, art they want to buy from a Claude, a Leonardo, a Rembrandt. No offense to Papa or grandpapa, but it works against me and I want—*I need*—every possible advantage to succeed. So I'm changing my name. But only my name, not my heritage."

"So, what's the name of a great painter?" his mother asked understandingly.

"Chagall. Marc Chagall," he declared. "That's a great artist's name… or at least it will be. *Someday.* I love you, Mama," he said kissing first his mother, then his baby sister on each cheek. "*Shalom.*"

"*Shalom… Monsieur Chagall,*" the old woman said with a smile, and then busied herself in the Sabbath preparations yet again.

"Aaron," Moishe called. "Hey, Aaron, where are you?"

"I'm right here, little brother" Aaron answered coming into the kitchen. "You ready to go?"

"Uh huh," Moishe answered in a low voice. "Look, I'm not—"

"Ah, I don't want to hear it. Fair is fair. Besides, I'll be fine. The institute in Moscow will take me. It's not as good as Berlin, but it's not chopped liver either and besides, it's free. Now go, before you miss the train and I have to share the bed with you another night. Eighteen years was enough," Aaron Siegel said and hugged his brother long and hard. "*Shalom…* Marc Chagall. *Shalom.*"

And at that, the painter kissed his mother on the forehead one last time, picked up his bag, and set off to make his way in the world.

. . . .

Twenty

"**Kozyolsk. Next stop, Kozyolsk,**" the conductor shouted as he walked through the third-class rail car. "Ko-zy-olsk." But, for as little attention the travelers crowded into the small railcar paid him, the conductor might as well have been naked. Instead, their gaze was fixed in awe at the old man seated at the center of the compartment. He had a thick shock of scraggly white beard hanging halfway down his chest, split almost neatly in two along a vertical fault beneath his chin, a broad nose with flaring nostrils, and his eyes, two, bright lumps of obsidian sparkled with every word he spoke.

It was as if the pope of the paupers was holding court. The old man sat at the center, swaddled in patched, woolen overclothes, underneath a threadbare blanket and scarf, and the peasants sat riveted from the floor to rafters, hanging onto their tribal chieftain's every word.

The old man's brow was beaded with sweat yet he shivered when he spoke. "Only then will you understand," he said in careful, measured tones. "You must give yourself up to God completely. He alone is the source of all goodness within you. Only then will you fully comprehend the intrinsic glory in such a thing as a good day's work in the fields. You will not only be intoxicated with life, you will be morally intoxicate—," the old man continued philosophizing, but his wheezing grew so fitful he could not go on.

"That's it, Lyovochka," a man declared from the seat beside him. "We're getting you off this train at the next stop and into the nearest bed."

"But—" the old man wheezed fitfully.

"No buts. I'm your doctor and I order it. We'll spend the night in Kozyolsk and in the morning we'll continue on to Shamordino. We will wire your sister from the station and tell her we will be delayed," he said, wiping the sweat from his patient's brow with an old handkerchief.

As the train slowed into the station, its bell ringing, the conductor called out from the stairway behind them, "Kozyolsk. Ko-zy-olsk."

"And now, ladies and gentlemen," the doctor said to the myriad frozen faces surrounding them, "You must excuse us."

As the pair made their way toward the door, applause broke out and the people began expressing their adoration, one by one.

"God bless you, Mr. Tolstoy," said one.

"To your health, Mr. Tolstoy," declared another.

"Long live Leopold Nicolayavich Tolstoy," several of them said.

The train finally rolled to a stop and the two men tottered down the steps onto the platform. And, as the doctor called for help from the railway attendants at one end of the third-class car, the newly minted Marc Chagall climbed aboard at the other.

The whistle blew, and the lumbering mass of metal lurched forward half an inch, then another, and another, until the morass of machinery slithered into the forest and was finally swallowed up around a curve just beyond the station's platform.

Standing behind her father, Hannah Kessler's hair glistened like honey in the warm afternoon light. As the sun melted behind the Moskvaskaya Mountains, her long, soft, curls shimmering in rhythm with the clickety-clack of the rails. She watched as Jacob Kessler held court, a crystal snifter of whiskey in one hand and a fat cigar in the other, Jacob Kessler looked every bit the monarch in a plush, purple velour chair at the head of the glass-enclosed observation deck perched above the first-class dining cabin. And why not, Hannah thought. Most of the people gathered around him might just as well have been his royal court.

To her father's left, Harry Lowenstein, the family's attorney and also her godfather. To his right, Jacob Kessler's lifeblood these past twenty-five years, his banker, Max Breslow. Next to Harry was Rose Ensler, widow of the department store magnate, Samuel Ensler, and Jacob's second cousin by marriage. Beside her, Kessler Insurance Company's biggest client, in more ways than one, Friedrich "Fritz" Kohlmann of Kohlmann Mining, and across from Fritz and all his chins, Friedrich, Jr., a gaunt twenty-seven-year-old who bore little resemblance to his father.

"What would your actuaries say to something like that, Jacob?" Fritz Kohlmann asked mockingly.

"You mean, would we insure it?" Jacob Kessler asked. "I'm not even sure I understand it. An automobile *factory*? Friedrich," he said turning to the pale young man, "why would you

117

even consider such a ludicrous business proposition? How many people are going to buy these things? How many can afford to? And for those who can, where are they going to go that they can't already go more easily, more comfortably, in a carriage or like we are now?" Jacob asked laughing, lifting his glass and taking a hearty sip.

But when the laughter died down, Friedrich still wanted to know, "Can it be insured or not?"

"Everything can be insured," Jacob Kessler answered. "But at what price? And what exactly are we insuring, that the factory won't go up in flames? That when people use these things and they smash into the side of a barn they won't come looking to you to repair the damages?"

"Can you imagine the law suits these automobiles will bring?" Harry Lowenstein asked.

"That's exactly what I'm saying," Jacob continued. "There are so many things to go wrong and so few opportunities to sell them. I don't see how you can even possibly pay the insurance premiums let alone make a profit. Mark my words, these automobiles will not last," Jacob Kessler declared finally.

"Thank you, Jacob. He needed to hear that from someone other than me," Fritz Kohlmann said.

"The price will come down," Friedrich said, still defending himself. "There's a guy in America, a Henryk Ford, he's building a factory to produce them by the thousands using a new system of moving conveyor belts."

"And there's a guy in the town square back in Radom who, for two rubles, will let you use his special telephone to talk to the Almighty," Max Breslow said sarcastically. "But even when he drops the price to one ruble on Sundays, still no one's buying," he laughed. "Stick with mining, *boychik*. Coal is the future, that's where the money is."

"Maybe for once, it's not just about money," Hannah blurted out.

At that, the group went silent, staring first at Hannah, then her father, until finally, Jacob Kessler asked, "Not about money? Can you imagine such a thing?" Then he burst into laughter, his court, save one, Rose Ensler, following suit.

"She's still young," the widow said, trying to soften the blow. "She'll learn."

"You think an automobile factory is bad, Fritzie," Jacob Kessler said. "You should have heard what my Hannah wanted to do."

Just then, with the last rays of sunlight crossing the horizon, the porter stepped up through the circular stairwell from below and rang the dinner bell in the observation lounge. "Dinner is served."

"*Mazel tov*," Jacob Kessler declared. "I'm starving. Let's eat."

One by one the group got up and made their way down the stairs. "Flowers. Can you believe your goddaughter, Harry? She was going to grow flowers for a living. Hannah, come along," he commanded as his head disappeared down the stairs, the sky behind her dissolving from its phosphorescent shades of burgundy into an inky black somewhere just beyond the horizon.

A quartet played Vivaldi's Four Seasons in one corner and with its white linen tablecloths, glittering crystal goblets, and polished silver, the first-class dining car was as elegantly appointed as any of the finest houses of haute cuisine Paris had to offer. Waiters in short white coats crinkled quietly as they served the ten or so tables in the car.

As always on these journeys, Jacob's table was by choice, the high-backed booth at the far corner and his guests huddled with him there now. Hannah took her place at her father's side and bowed her head for the blessings.

Jacob Kessler took the urn of water out of the small silver bowl it was placed in in front of him and began pouring the water three times over each hand from the urn into the bowl, first the right hand, then the left, then the right again, as he recited the blessing over the washing of the hands in Hebrew. *"Baruch atah Adonai, Elohaynu Melech ha olam, a sher kid a shanu be mitzvo tav, v'tzi vanu al ti lat ya da yim.* Blessed are you, Lord, our God, King of the Universe who sanctifies us through His commandments and commanded us concerning the elevation of the hands." Then, without hesitation, Jacob recited the blessing over the wine. *Ba-ruch atah Adonai Elohaynu Melech ha olam, borei p'ri hagafen.* Blessed are You, Lord, our God, King of the Universe, who creates the fruit of the vine." At which, Jacob and the others took a sip from their cups. Finally, Jacob gave thanks for the bread. *"Baruch atah Adonoi, Eloheinu Melech ha olam, ha motzi lechem min ha aretz.* Blessed are You, Lord, our God, King of the Universe, who brings forth bread from the Earth. Amen."

"Amen," the group responded vigorously as Jacob broke the loaf of bread and passed pieces of it around the table.

"So, Rose," Jacob Kessler began, "Did I hear right, you're stopping in Prague for a few days?"

"I bought some property there, yes." Nearing seventy, Rose Ensler had aged well, gracefully with a good complexion and strong, grayish-green eyes that set off nicely against her thick hair, that only now started to be as much gray as black. Something in the way Rose Ensler carried herself let you know that she was warm and approachable, yet, at the same time she was not one who could be easily taken advantage of.

"A nice flat for the summers," Jacob asked. "Something on the river, perhaps close to the theaters?"

"Not quite," Rose said coyly. "We're looking at locations here."

"Locations?" Jacob asked. "What do you mean?"

"You're going to open another store?" Harry Lowenstein asked incredulously.

"Maybe," Rose said, taking another sip of wine. "Yes," she finally admitted.

"Ten of the biggest department stores in Poland aren't enough?" Max Breslow added.

"Sam always used to say 'When you're in business, standing still is the same as moving backwards.'"

"Yes, but Rose," Jacob pleaded. "Sam was—"

"What? *Say it*," Rose Ensler implored him. "Sam was what? A man?"

"That's not it."

"Look, it's been six years since Sam passed. Who do you think has been running the stores since? And who do you think sat beside him running those stores for forty-five years before that?"

"That's not it at all—" Jacob Kessler started.

"Ensler's has an opportunity to expand into a strong market and I'm going to take it. If you don't want to insure it," she said to Jacob, "and you don't want to fund it," she told Max, "and you don't want to represent it," she told Harry Lowenstein, "that's fine. There are plenty of others who will."

"What are you getting so upset for, Rose?" Jacob said doggedly. "I just meant it's getting a little late in your life—in all our lives—to start taking on new headaches like this. Managing ten stores is tough enough let alone managing ten stores in one place and building and opening a new one five hundred kilometers away."

"Two," Rose said plainly.

"It's not two hundred kilometers from Radom to Prague--"

"Stores. We're opening two *stores*. There's a need for one near the square and also further down by the castle. I'm not going to sit by and leave a hole only to have Glickman come in and take fifty percent of my market."

"*Oy*," Harry, Max, and Jacob sighed in unison.

"Lord knows I could never persuade Sam to stop growing the business either. Thank God," Jacob finally relented warmly. "Okay, Rose, if it's what you really want, of course we'll do it."

Just then, everyone's attention was drawn to a commotion brewing midway through the dining car where the waiters had cornered an intruder.

"Alright, stop. It was a mistake. I'm sorry," Marc Chagall explained hastily as the staff hemmed him in. "I thought this was the way to the baggage car."

122

The maitre d' reached for the young man's arm to escort him out, but the train bolted sharply to one side. In response, the wheels screeched and ground against the rails sending the young man, and a fair amount of tableware, tumbling through the car. When the tracks finally straightened out, Chagall found himself on the far end of the car, tangled arm in arm with Hannah who had been knocked to the floor.

As he got up, Chagall's eyes locked onto the beautiful creature beside him, and Hannah Kessler sat there, stunned, and breathing in quick, shallow breaths. He began to look her up and down, but as his eyes met hers, his gaze became fixed at the two radiant fields of blue staring back at him. His jaw dropped, his lips parted weakly, and he melted into her eyes. "Oh my lord," he whispered under his breath.

"Excuse me?" Hannah asked.

Chagall leapt up, pulling Hannah along with him. "I'm so sorry. Please excuse me, Miss," he apologized. "Are you alright?"

Before she could answer, the waiters had regrouped and once again took custody of Chagall, begging Hannah's—and Jacob's—forgiveness in the process. "Please accept our apologies, Mr. Kessler. This will never happen again, Miss Kessler," they bleated sheepishly.

As the servers pressed against him, Chagall twisted himself free. "I said I was going," he told them then dusted himself off. Then, turning toward Hannah, he asked, "Are you sure you're alright, Miss?"

Hannah drank him in. His lean farmer's frame, a strong neck between a pair of broad shoulders, and thick, springy legs that seemed more than sturdy now. Underneath Chagall's dark navy cap she saw a thick mop of pale, honey-colored hair—feathers really—lighting out in every direction. And when the young painter lifted his head, Hannah felt his eyes—those soft pools of grayish blue—lock on to hers and her spine veritably tingled. "Yes," she barely whispered.

Chagall drank her in some more, then, after a moment, nodded his head, tipped his hat, and turned to leave. But before the young man reached the door, the maitre d' put a hand on his shoulder and turned him back around one more time. As Chagall looked at him, the dining captain turned his gaze toward the man's loose-fitting, almost burlap-like pants and the round bulge in one pocket. A moment later, Chagall produced a bread roll. Handing it back he said slyly, "It must have rolled in there," then turned to go again.

As the headwaiter was about to show the man the door, Jacob Kessler called out, "Wait. Oscar, bring him here, please." At that, the dining captain turned himself and his young charge abruptly around and marched to the corner booth.

The group watched silently as Jacob Kessler assessed the vagrant, grinding those eyes of his up and down the young man, as if staring through to his very soul. Finally, he stroked his beard and slowly split apart his lips. "Please," he said softly, "accept my apologies."

Chagall stood motionless, stunned for the moment by the act of contrition, while beside him, the maitre d' began to grow flush with embarrassment.

"You made a simple mistake coming in here, and then there's a curve in our path, and the next thing you know, you're a criminal being escorted out by the authorities. It doesn't seem right," he said, glancing at the Star of David dangling on a chain around his neck. "Will you join us for dinner, Mister…?

"Sieg—" the painter began, then corrected himself, "Chagall, Marc Chagall, " he said dusting himself off some more and straightening his clothes. "And yes. I'd be delighted to join you, thank you very much."

"Oscar, set a place for Mr. Chagall," Jacob Kessler ordered, and the group squeezed in around the table to make room for one more opposite Friedrich Jr. and beside Hannah.

"This will be interesting," Friedrich, Jr. said sarcastically turning to Rose Ensler.

When he finished the introductions, Jacob Kessler turned to his new guest, poured him a glass of wine, and asked, "So, Mr. Chagall, besides a flawed sense of direction, an overzealous train engineer, and a rather serendipitous curve in the rail lines, what else brings you this way today?"

"Well, since you put it that way," Chagall said with a smile, "I guess I would have to say, the hand of God."

"Oh?" Jacob asked. "How's that?"

So the young man explained about his brother, the race, and the bet, and they all listened intently, Hannah especially.

"Besides the hand of God," Chagall concluded, "how else could someone like me, who, just hours ago was a pauper peeling potatoes and pickling cucumbers, suddenly find himself sitting down to this magnificent meal with you extraordinary people on my way to Paris to become a famous painter?" At that, he swigged down his wine and thrust his goblet in front of Friedrich, Jr. to be filled and asked smartly, "Right, Friedrich?"

"Right," Friedrich, Jr. replied weakly as he poured.

"To the hand of God," Chagall raised his glass and toasted.

"To the hand of God," they all agreed heartily as they drank up and then dug into the exquisite meal now set out before them.

"How can you say that?" Chagall asked with conviction, emptying a third bottle of wine into his goblet, the table in front of him littered with enough empty dishes and plates to have fed a platoon of starving artists. "Professor Masaryk is certain to save the Czechs. You must be a Realist."

"Mr. Chagall," Hannah explained, "You forget. My father is in the insurance business. He is the ultimate realist."

"I mean, come on, the Young Czechs. Justice. Morality," Chagall continued. "Common decency for everyone regardless of which day a man calls the Sabbath. These are principles everyone can subscribe to. Between the strength of the Realist party and the frailty of the throne, Masaryk has to succeed sooner or later."

"Unless they defenestrate him too," Jacob Kessler chided.

"Throw him out a window?" Chagall asked.

"It wouldn't be the first time in Czech politics an opponent met with an untimely fall from a second or third story, would it?"

"But look at how Masaryk helped Hilsner," Chagall said.

"That's your idea of help, Mr. Chagall, life in prison?" Harry Lowenstein asked.

"Considering the alternative, yes."

"If an innocent man getting life in prison is good fortune, then we are all doomed," Fritz Kohlmann said.

"He's not through with the appeals yet," Chagall said. "You'll see. First he reverses the death penalty, then soon enough Hilsner will be dancing in Wenceslaus Square."

"You must forgive my father, Mr. Chagall," Hannah apologized. "He sees the worst in everyone and everything."

"I see the truth," Jacob Kessler defended himself. "The truth."

"Enough with these morbid political discussions," Rose Ensler said, changing the topic. "So, you're going to become a painter, Mr. Chagall. That sounds fascinating. Whose work do you find especially interesting today?"

"Have you seen some of the things put out by this new fellow, what's his name, Max Breslow asked, "Picasso, and some of his friends? *Oy*, everything out of place, and upside down, and in inverse proportions."

"Noses where ears should be, eyeballs in bellybuttons," Harry Lowenstein said. "What do they call themselves, cubists?"

"I call them confused-ists," Jacob Kessler joked.

"Where will you study?" Hannah wanted to know.

"I've got my application in at La Palette," Chagall answered.

"La Palette," Friedrich, Jr. repeated. "That's a very expensive institution. Will they admit someone like you? I mean someone…who can't pay the fees?"

"I can pay—" Chagall started.

"Getting into art school is not like going into business, dear," Rose Ensler shot back drolly. "It doesn't take money. It takes talent."

"Artists don't measure people by their wealth alone," Hannah added.

"No, of course not," Friedrich agreed all too easily. "Not until it's time to sell their work. Then suddenly a man's character and taste is judged by the size of his bank account. Isn't that right, Mr. Chagall?"

"Yes," Marc replied bluntly. "But sometimes, in inverse proportions," he said with a wry smile.

It took a moment, but the sarcasm in Chagall's remark finally sank in with the group, and when Jacob Kessler laughed they all laughed. "Very good, Mr. Chagall. Very good," indeed. "Shall we repair to the observation lounge?"

"Cognac and cigars, upstairs," Rose Ensler whispered in Chagall's ear.

"Mr. Chagall, will you join us?" Jacob Kessler asked.

"Sure…" Chagall began. But then, out of the corner of his eye, he caught sight of Hannah slipping out the door at the rear of the dining car. "I'd like to, but I think I should be getting back. Thank you for everything, Mr. Kessler," he said putting down his napkin, then quickly turned for the door.

"Well, best of luck to you," Jacob said.

"Yes," the others added as he left.

"Thank you. Thank you very much," Marc Chagall said excusing himself.

Chagall worked his way down the train, car by car to the very last one, where he found Hannah, one foot on the bottom step of the caboose, the other dangling over the edge as the tracks spooled out in two shiny ribbons behind her, the sound of the clickety-clack, clickety-clack along the rails filling the air around them as the train surged through a canyon in the bright, moonlit night.

"If you can wait just a few more minutes, the landing is much softer," the artist told Hannah, startling her. The wind was blowing her shiny blonde hair back and a full moon hung low and large behind her in the inky black sky, a million, million stars sparkling all around it. "There's a lake a few kilometers down the tracks. At least wait until then," he said, reaching for her.

"Get back, I'll jump," she warned and moved closer to the edge.

"I didn't say 'Don't jump,' I said 'Wait.' I think you should jump, you just should wait a few minutes is all."

"You think I *should* jump?" Hannah Kessler asked curiously clinging to the handrails.

"Absolutely."

"Oh? Why is that?"

"Your life stinks. I heard what your father has in mind for you. You're not the type who's going to be happy calculating the odds of someone slipping on a patch of ice or how many people— to the nearest tenth of a human life will die in any given year. It's not you."

"And how would you know?" Hannah asked, annoyed at his impertinence. "Because you spent an hour drinking my father's wine, eating my father's food? You don't know me."

"You're right. I don't," the painter answered, his eyes gleaming in the moonlight. "But I know sadness when I see it. The kind of sadness that hurts deep down inside. And confusion. And... pain. You won't be happy running an insurance business," he said reaching for her hand, "but surely there's another alternative." He looked her straight in the eye and said, "Sit," then sat himself down on the top step. "Please," he pleaded gently. "There's time until the lake comes up. I'll tell you, I promise."

Hannah hesitated a moment, then moved a little closer to him. "I just sat there at dinner and watched my whole life play out before me. Over and over. Endless board meetings and stuffy dinners with clients. 'The return on investment is eight point three percent,' she said in a mocking voice. 'We're going to have to amortize it over twenty years,'" she continued. "So much useless chitchat doled out over caviar and cognac. I can't bring myself to do it for the rest of my life. I *won't*."

"So, don't do it. But that doesn't mean you have to jump off the back of a speeding train and split your head open on some rocks, does it? Back home in Vitebsk—that's where I'm from by the way, in Russia—we have this huge hill down by the Vitba River near where the old fortress used to be. Well, in the winter, especially when it freezes over like it did last night, the hill gets icy and, if you're not careful on the way home from Friday night services at the synagogue," he explained, "you can slip down the hillside and fall headfirst into the large pieces of rock that split off from the fort little by little each year. It really hurts, let me tell you.

130

I've done it," he said leaning over and, putting his hands to his head to show her the scar underneath his scalp. "And my brother Aaron, well, he did it twice and he's supposed to be the smarter one of the two of us. It's no picnic, let me tell you," he said.

"Leave me alone," Hannah snapped.

"Look, all I'm saying is, you seem to be an intelligent person—"

"What's that supposed to mean?" she huffed. "'I *seem* to be an intelligent person?' How dare you?"

"Well, not to overstate the obvious, Miss Kessler, but that was your caboose dangling off the rear end of this caboose, was it not?" He watched as the irony settled in on her, then reached out his hand. After taking one more look out over the back of train, she accepted, then pulled herself up. "That's better. Come on, let's talk about your options," Marc Chagall said smiling and standing up.

"Okay," she answered and moved to join him. As she did, the train's whistle blew sharply into the night air and the train swerved hard again. In an instant, Hannah Kessler lost her footing, nearly falling off the train completely were it not for the young artist diving after her to grab her wrist. Chagall held her, dangling inches above the rails as the train sped along, hugging the sheer side of a cliff that plunged a thousand feet into a dark canyon below. Hannah shrieked and Chagall tightened his grip even further.

"I've got you," he shouted as the screeching wheels pierced the air and her cries echoed through the abyss below. "Stop screaming. I've got you. Pay attention and pull yourself up with your other arm. You can do this," he told her firmly, holding the handrail with one hand and Hannah with the other.

After a moment, Hannah reached up, took hold of a metal clamp and began pulling herself up until finally she had a steady footing and Chagall could pull her back onto the platform.

As he put her safely back onto the platform, their eyes locked together and he held her tight, so tightly it seemed as though their hearts beat as one, until, suddenly, the train screeched to a halt.

When they looked up Marc Chagall and Hannah Kessler found themselves surrounded by a posse of people, beginning with her father and his court, and ending with half a dozen railroad employees who immediately grabbed Hannah and thrust her into Jacob Kessler's arms. Then they turned to Chagall and pulled his arms stiffly behind him and handcuffed him.

"I see we meet again," the conductor barked coldly.

"What is the meaning of this?" Jacob Kessler shouted. "Are you okay?" he turned and asked his daughter, who quickly nodded yes.

"Answer him!" the conductor commanded Chagall.

"I… I…" the young man stumbled to explain. But before he could, Hannah chimed in.

"I… I came out here to look at the stars and when we went around that last curve a few minutes ago, I lost my footing. Then Marc, Mr. Chagall, came by and saved me," Hannah said looking into her father's furious eyes until finally, he accepted what she said and gave her a hug. "Thank God."

"Is that the way of it?" the conductor demanded, squeezing the young man's arm and rousting him.

Chagall looked up at Hannah, the moonlight sparkling in her eyes, her long blonde hair blowing gently in the cold night air, then quietly said, "Yes."

"Well, then," Rose Ensler declared. "The boy's a hero. He saved Hannah's life. Bravo, young man. Bravo," she said, pumping his hand vigorously.

"Here, here," they all agreed except for Jacob.

"Well, Mr. Chagall," Jacob Kessler said. "It seems I am in your debt."

"It's nothing," the painter said.

"So tell us, Mr. Chagall," Fritz, Jr. asked, "do you have a long history of heroic deeds or is it just timing and good fortune conjoining in your life again as it did when you first stumbled our way?"

Chagall shot a quick glance over to Hannah but with her head tilted down, the young woman provided no guidance as to how he should respond.

"How is it that you happened to be all the way back here in the first place… and at just the right moment?" Fritz, Jr. wanted to know. "Not an hour ago, you were but a fly on the windowpane of our world, the outside of the windowpane at that, and now, all of a sudden, thanks to the hand of God as you put it, wherever we turn, it seems there you are, buzzing about."

Put that way the group all stared at Chagall until finally Hannah jumped in. "He wasn't back here to begin with. He heard my screams and came running." she declared. Then she looked at Chagall, who, after a moment, slowly nodded yes. "I'm grateful he came along when he did. And you should be too," Hannah chided Fritz, Jr..

"I couldn't agree more," Rose Ensler said heartily.

"Well, there you have it," Max Breslow declared. "It's a good thing he came along when he did. The lad's a hero, so let's all go in and celebrate and warm up with a nice glass of schnapps." And so, they all turned and filed back into the rail car, leaving only Chagall on the platform with Jacob, Hannah, and Harry Lowenstein.

"Thank you, Mr. Chagall," Jacob said rather unconvincingly. As he turned to leave with Hannah, Harry grabbed Jacob Kessler's arm and whispered into his ear. A moment later, Jacob Kessler nodded quietly, took Hannah's elbow and left. Then Harry Lowenstein took out a fifty-ruble banknote and tucked it into the artist's hand. "Mr. Kessler wishes to express his appreciation."

'Hey, I don't need any chari—"

"A little something for the tuition perhaps, or some art supplies? You're not exactly there on a full scholarship, are you?" Harry said, then turned and left.

"Friedrich will come to his senses soon enough," Jacob Kessler told his daughter as they sat in the plush sitting room of their private sleeping car. "He will make a good businessman like his father one day, you'll see."

"What's that supposed to mean?" Hannah asked as she slipped out of her shoes.

"What do you think it means? Someday he will be a good businessman like his father," Jacob answered, then he stood up and began putting out the lights one by one.

"Not that part," Hannah said, getting up too. "The part about 'you'll see.'"

"You'll see means you'll see, Channelah." Jacob said firmly.

"Don't Channelah me. 'You'll see' means you have something up your sleeve, Papa. Oh," she began fuming after a minute. "Don't tell me—"

"I meant Friedrich will become a good businessman like his father and, as his insurer you will benefit from that greatly," Jacob Kessler said, snuffing out all but the last light, leaving them in the dim glow of a single lamp.

"You didn't say it in your Jacob Kessler insurance-man voice, you said it in your papa-voice, that same tone of voice you used when you told me about going to the institute."

"What's so terrible if we keep the Kohlmann account in the family another generation?"

"In the family? Papa, tell me you didn't—" she said, her voice rising.

"Didn't what? Make sure you're taken care of, no matter what?"

"You promised me to Friedrich, Jr.?!" she asked, outraged. "How could you? Without so much as even consulting me? We don't need their money, Papa. We have plenty of money. How could you…?" she turned away and started sobbing.

"It's not just about money, Channelah," he said, trying to calm her down. "A person needs more than money, you know that. Especially…"

"Especially what? For a *woman*, that's what you were going to say, isn't it?"

Jacob Kessler walked over to Hannah and gently put his large hands on her slender shoulders. He walked around in front of her and knelt down. Then he looked into his daughter's tear-filled eyes and held her softly. "Yes," he finally whispered. "No matter what you do, society doesn't accept women in business."

"You mean men don't accept women because they don't want to give up their power," she said.

"Maybe so, but it is what it is. Look at Rose. She stood by Sam's side his entire life in the business. Everyone saw the contributions she made, but still, now that he's gone, it's a different story entirely."

"She seems to do fine," Hannah said abruptly.

"Yes, she seems to. But it's been very difficult. Why do you think she's opening two new stores in Prague? Because she wants to? To beat Glickman out of a new market? No. She's losing two stores in Warsaw and another in Cracow because the landlords won't renew the leases. Why? Because she's a woman. No other reason. The stores make money, they've paid their leases on time for forty years straight."

"That's not fair," Hannah protested. "Can't she do something? Can't you talk to them? Can't Uncle Harry sue them?"

"There's nothing to sue over. They're not breaking the leases or the law. The leases have expired and the landlords own the buildings. They can do whatever they want," he said slowly shaking his head. Then, raising it back again and taking her gently by the chin, he said, "And it won't be any easier for you, my Channelah. You'll need someone like Friedrich to keep the wolves at bay." Then he planted a kiss on his daughter's forehead and put out the last light, leaving her only the moonlight and the clickety-clack of the rails by which to ponder those heavy thoughts as she cried herself to sleep.

. . . .

Twenty-one

The train pulled into the Prague Central Station that next morning in a cacophonous burst of hissing steam and grinding metal. As it ground to a halt, a herd of porters descended on the platform in a swarm. When the rail cars finally rolled to a final stop, the conductor and the dining captain jumped down onto the platform and set out the step stool at the foot of the stairs outside the first-class car. Then they stood at attention and helped the passengers down one by one.

"You know," Jacob Kessler said, turning to Harry Lowenstein behind him as he stepped off the train, "I'm a little concerned about the Balkans. Things there still aren't settled." Then turning back around, he placed a generous tip in each of their hands as he took it for support. "Thank you very much."

"Thank *you*, sir," the conductor said smartly, then reached up to help Lowenstein, and finally, Hannah, down the steps. "Thank *you*, Mr. Lowenstein. Miss Kessler, please accept my apologies. I'm sorry you had such a difficult journey with us this time. I assure you—"

"Thank you," Hannah said somewhat distractedly and she turned away from him. Instead, she gazed down the length of the train as it discharged its cargoes, human, animal, and otherwise.

"Stay here, Channeleh, I'm going to check on the carriage with Harry. Then I'm going to see what that moron Kafka is up to and we'll go home."

"Yes, Papa."

"It's been two years since Vienna annexed Bosnia and Herzegovina," Harry Lowenstein said reassuringly as they walked away. "Things have been quiet, more or less."

"How long do you think the Tsar will let things stay that way?" Jacob asked.

"They're mostly Serbs there, I don't think he cares that much about them."

"He doesn't. But that doesn't mean he doesn't have a reputation to protect."

"The Hapsburgs don't want a war with the Romanovs," Harry Lowenstein assured him. "Austria-Hungary is not prepared to take on the Russians. Franz Joseph doesn't want a war with Nicholas. Not a full-scale one anyway. Maybe some border skirmishes but nothing like before."

"Maybe Franz Joseph doesn't, but I'm not so sure about that kid of his. That Franz Ferdinand is a loose arrow. You wait, one day he's going to provoke somebody into a mess over something positively idiotic and if the Germans chime in, the end result is not going to be pretty."

Hannah watched as her father and uncle melted into the crowd, then turned back around and starting searching through the disembarking passengers as they moved past her. Finally, in the distance, she saw what she was looking for, amidst the cargo of cackling chickens and honking geese: the young artist dusting off his baggy trousers and trying vainly to restrain his mop of hair under his cap as he walked in her direction.

As Chagall finally moved past her, Hannah Kessler lightly grazed his shoulder with her white-gloved hand, and said, "Excuse me, Mr. Chagall?"

"Oh, Miss Kessler," the young man said with a start. "Hello again. Or is it goodbye?"

"I…just wanted to say…thank you," Hannah said haltingly. "For yesterday. For your help and your… discretion."

"It's alright," he said, tilting his head down. "You would've done the same, I'm sure. We all get stretched a little thin sooner or later."

"I don't know what came over me. It got to a point where I couldn't breathe anymore. I thought I would die if I couldn't grow my flowers and had to stay in the insurance business the rest of my life. But, I'm alright now, it won't be so bad. Anyway, that's all I wanted to say. Thank you."

"Well, actually, now I don't know," Chagall said curiously. "That *does* sound pretty bad."

"What?" Hannah asked, a bit confused.

"When you put it that way, it sounds horrible," Chagall continued. "Now that I know what I know, I would have done the same as you. I'm sorry, I probably shouldn't have interfered."

"Excuse me? Are you suggesting that you should have let me, you know… go?" Hannah asked, more than a little shocked.

"No, of course not."

"Because that's sure what it sounded like you suggested."

"I meant that all that insurance nonsense sounds terrible and I would have fought to find a way out of it too; albeit a

140

smarter, less dangerous way perhaps, but a way out all the same. But, that's the thing about trying to run away from your problems," he said with a wry grin. "Sooner or later you run out of places to run to. And eventually you discover there is no place to hide from yourself and there never was."

"Well," Hannah chafed. "I'm resigned to it now, and I'm going to do a damned fine job of it."

"Of course, you will," he said, a hint of sarcasm in his tone.

"I will."

"Because your father said you will."

"What?!" Hannah said angrily as she stepped out in front of an oncoming cart, forcing it to go around her. "This has nothing to do with my father. How dare you even suggest such a thing. This was my decision entirely."

"Then why did you just do that?"

"Do what?"

"Step over there the way you did."

"I didn't do anything," she said in a low voice putting her head down. Then, after a moment, "It would've been crushed," she said looking down at the small blossom coming up through the pavement cracks she had saved by stepping out into the path of the baggage cart.

"It most certainly would have. But most people wouldn't even notice it, let alone care, or take the time to do something about it."

"So?" Hannah said, miffed.

"So, you're someone who needs to celebrate life and all its beauty every day, not someone who will be content calculating its all-too-certain tragedies and maladies from dawn until dusk."

"How can you say that? You had one dinner with me and you think you know me?"

"I can see it in your eyes," Marc Chagall said plainly. "Anyone can. Anyone who's paying attention that is."

At that last statement Hannah put her head down.

"I'm sorry, I didn't mean to say that. I'm sure your father means well."

"I want to grow flowers," she said meekly. "But of course Papa says that's no way to make a living. He doesn't understand."

"You were going to jump off that train and leave everything—the money, the clothing, the homes, the meals—to do what? Grow flowers? Are you *meshugah*?"

"No, I am not *meshugah*, whatever that means."

"You don't speak Yiddish?"

"Papa won't allow it. He says it's a bastard language used only by uncultured, gutter Je—" she said before she could stop herself. "Oh my, I'm sorry. I didn't mean to imply…"

"That's okay. I know what side of the tracks I came from," Chagall said without taking offense. "Well, anyway, *meshugah* means crazy. And, trust me, I am *meshugah* and I know crazy when I see it. You never said anything about wanting to grow flowers for a living. Your father is right. No one can make a living that way. I thought he was condemning you to a life of fiscal drudgery and keeping you from dancing with the ballet, or singing opera. I thought he was keeping you from running off with the circus or a band of gypsies. But flowers?"

142

"My flowers will be the best," she pleaded, her eyes lighting up and her voice growing more excited and her speech getting faster and faster until the words ran together. "Their stems will grow greener and straighter, their scents will dance across the room and awaken the senses like no other. Their colors will gleam like nothing you've ever seen.

"Whoa, whoa, whoa. Slow down," Chagall said with a big smile. "You're talking so fast I can hardly understand you."

'Everyone will want my flowers. Kings and queens, presidents and prime ministers, will order my bouquets for their finest state dinners. Brides will dream of Hannah Kessler providing the flowers for their weddings."

"Well," Chagall laughed in a warm voice, "maybe you're right. My father told me the same thing. 'Painting houses is hardly a living, let alone painting pictures,'" the young man chortled, imitating his father. He held his father's comically stern pose until Hannah cracked first a smile, then finally, a short burst of laughter. "Just before I was thirteen, before my bar mitzvah, I remember telling him all about the masters. Rembrandt, Da Vinci, Goya. How I will do what they did and more. How I would convince the world with my canvases. How I will be at least as famous as them, maybe more. You know what his response was?"

Hannah smiled and shook her head no.

"You can't eat fame," he said continuing to mock his father. "I know from this Da Vinci. He died without a single kopek in his pocket."

"So what did you do?"

"I left for St. Petersburg, what else could I do?"

"And?"

"And, I went as far as I could go there. Then, I came home."

"Is that some of your work?" she asked, pointing to the small book he carried under his arm.

"Yes."

"May I?" she asked, reaching for the leather case.

"Sure," he said handing it over. He watched as she opened the journal and perused his work. The first piece was a subdued portrait of a young girl on a sofa, her thick brown hair cropped short under her black cap, one leg crooked up and crossed over the other. "That's my sister, Mariaska, well, Marussio really, but we all call her Mariaska. She's about eight there." Then, she flipped to the next one, a smaller, more abstract and colorful painting with broad, bold strokes of reds and yellows, blues and greens, depicting a woman selling fruit. Then the next one, darker in tone, showed a village street with a man lying on it. Surrounding him, half a dozen lit candelabras. And on the prow of the roof of one of the small, brownish hovels, a man on playing a fiddle. "That's my uncle. He's not so good. It's the only place my aunt will let him play," he said with a smile.

"These are very, very good," Hannah cooed as she continued flipping through his work, until she came to one of a woman, nude, seated against the trunk of a tree and smiling warmly. "Oh my," she said, a little shocked.

"That's Thea. She's just a friend."

"Hmm…" Hannah said pursing her lips and perusing page after page of Thea. Thea lying on a sofa, her body folding perfectly into the soft arch in the divan; Thea, straight on, her breasts like two soft, pink bowls; Thea, her back to them, her arms and legs wrapped around the front of the chair, her lithe, curvaceous body a veritable human cello. "A very good friend, apparently."

"Actually, yes," he said earnestly.

"These are exquisite," she said closing the portfolio. "You're very talented."

"Thank you."

"I've been doing the same thing," Hannah said in an anxious smile. "Oh," she said then quickly realizing what she said, she blushed and added, "Not posing like that. I mean, I've been teaching myself about flowers in secret. I memorize one new species a day. I study their Latin names, what type of soil they like, how much water and how much acidity they need in their soil, what climate they prefer, whether they do best in sun or shade, everything. I have over five thousand memorized so far."

"I guess that's okay," Chagall said dryly.

"What's that supposed to mean?"

"Well, I suppose, if you're going to insure flowers it's important. But how often do you think that's going to happen? It's fine that you have a good memory. It'll help with your actuarial tables. Otherwise..." he trailed off.

"Otherwise, what?" she demanded in a tightening tone.

Marc Chagall hesitated, thought about his response for a moment, and then, went with his original thought. "Otherwise...what's the point? If you're not going to actually follow your dreams, I mean. Back home they'd say that's just a party trick."

"A what?!" Hannah fumed. "A party trick?"

"I didn't say *I* would say that," Chagall said backpedaling. "I said, 'they' would say that. You know, other people. Not me," he continued backpedaling, with little success.

"Oh no, I think it's quite clear who said what, but... it's the truth," she finally admitted weakly.

"Sometimes it's not enough to just want to do things," he explained gently. "Sometimes you actually have to do them."

The words stung but Hannah Kessler realized she couldn't dispute their validity. "Who am I kidding? You're right," she conceded. "I talk about growing flowers but the reality is I'm here in Prague ready to enroll at the institute. Why can't I be more like you, more independent? More like a man. Men don't have these issues. They just do what they want to do whenever they want to do it. You wanted to go to St. Petersburg, you picked yourself up and went to St. Petersburg. You wanted to go to Paris and here you are. Men never get bogged down by the consequences. They see something they want, they go after it. They're so free and easy."

"You can do that. To be free, all you've got to do is *think free*. It's all up here," he said, tapping his index finger against his forehead.

"I don't think I know how to do that."

"Then, I'll teach you," Chagall said, looking her straight in the eye.

"You'd do that?" she asked, her eyes lighting up, and her wide smile revealing those beautiful, white teeth. "You'd teach me to run like a man?"

"Sure."

"And drink like a man?" she asked, laughing.

"Of course. We can go to Paris together and drink Sangria in Montmartre and run through the fountains until we're soaked through and the gendarmes come and haul us away."

"And you'll teach me to forget all about my manners and belch like a wild boar in the middle of the boulevard at high noon?"

"On the Champs Elysee-e-e-e-e-e-e-e-e," Chagall belched out in a big, laughing burp. "But we can do that right now," he said taking her by the arm and pulling her behind a stack of luggage piled up on the platform behind them. "I'll show you."

"No, Marc," she said, tugging back and giggling.

"S-u-r-r-r-re, right now," he belched again and continued tugging. "Come on,"

She tried resisting once more but then Hannah relented as he pulled her behind the suitcases.

"It comes from here," he said pointing at the hollow of his throat. "You've just got to suck it in and then let yourself go." Then he pressed at the hollow, sucked in his esophagus, and let out an enormous burp. "Now you try."

He watched as Hannah put her hand to her neck and searched for the spot to press in. Chagall took her soft, delicate gloved hand in his and gently guided it to the right spot. "There," he said, soaking in her sweet scent. "Now, suck it back, kind of a like a turtle pulling its head in and then set it free."

Hannah pushed and pulled at her throat, then sucked in a gulp of air and grimaced until finally a tiny, dainty belch came out. "I did it," she said proudly.

"That's a good start, but you've got to get more air behind it. Like this," he explained, sticking out his chest and hauling back

147

and letting another monster roar from his throat. "You have to feel it way back here," he said as if reaching down his throat with his hand.

Hannah began to concentrate, positioning her feet shoulder width apart and adjusting her stance. She clasped her hands in front of her like a diva, pursed her lips, sucked in an ocean of air in a giant whoosh and then Hannah Kessler threw her head back and ultimately released a rather formidable belch. "Wow," she laughed.

"That's it, you got it now," Chagall said, laughing. He let another one rip and Hannah responded in kind, until they went at it like a pair of bullfrogs in heat.

"Burrrrrp."

"Buuuurrrrp."

"Burrrrp."

"Burrrrrrrrrrp."

"What is that horrible croaking?" Jacob Kessler demanded as he and Harry Lowenstein returned. "And where is Channeleh?" Then, from behind the pile of suitcases, he heard, "That's good, but let's see you beat this one." And then the two men walked around behind them.

Hannah watched as her father and uncle came around and took up a position behind Chagall. Before she could say anything, the young artist let wail with a rip-roaring masterpiece of a belch.

"Now *that* was a work of art, eh?" he asked her. "Come on, admit it, that was pretty good. You won't be able to top that, will you?"

Hannah Kessler didn't answer, instead putting her head down. "Father. You remember Mr. Chagall?"

"Yes, of course," Jacob Kessler said flatly as the artist turned around sheepishly.

"Excuse me, sir," Chagall said, red-faced. "I didn't realize—"

Jacob Kessler smiled weakly, then turned to Hannah and said, "Kafka has the bags all taken care of. Shall we go? Nice seeing you again Mr. Chagall," he said taking Hannah's hand and turned to leave. "Good luck in Paris."

"Thank you, sir. But I don't think I'll be headed there just yet."

"Oh?" Jacob asked warily as he stopped and turned back.

"There are some interesting things going on here in Prague. Artistically, I mean. I was reading about it here in the paper," he said, pulling out a folded up journal from his coat pocket. "There's a movement here called Skupina, and they are taking modernism in some very interesting directions. Some are calling them the Czech cubists, but they are the new avant-garde and they've established a little network here."

"So you'll be staying in Prague, then?" Hannah asked, a trace of hopefulness in her voice.

"Yes."

"Where will you stay?"

"I'll stay where I am, until I'm not," he said, smiling. "I'll bale hay and sleep in the barn or chop wood and stay in the shed. Either way, I'll be fine."

"Very well, yes. Good day, Mr. Chagall," Jacob Kessler said stiffly, taking his daughter's arm, and walking away.

149

Chagall watched and waited until finally Hannah Kessler turned and looked back at him and smiled. He took off his cap, letting his feathers fly loose, and bowed deeply at the waist. Then, in broad, exaggerated movements, he straightened up and mouthed, "Think free."

What? she asked with her eyes.

"Think free!" he shouted into the air, laughing and running the other way, smiling at the onlookers who watched as he leapt away, kicking up his heels every step of the way.

Hannah smiled and then turned back to continue on with her father.

"Please, Hannah," Jacob Kessler said sternly. "Let's get on with it."

"Yes, Papa," she said, her head turned down, her smile as wide as could be.

. . . .

Twenty-two

The moonlight spilling in the window behind her, one by one, Hannah Kessler rearranged the items on top of her dresser in her bedroom, her every move reflected in the large, gilded mirror hanging above the chest of drawers. She took her ivory hairbrush and put it where the small portrait of her mother was standing. Then, she moved her mother next to the porcelain vase full of flowers she had picked and arranged earlier that day positioning it so the moonlight caught her mother's eyes and her smile, and the silver in the frame shined around Libby Kessler like a halo.

Hannah smoothed down the lace doily on the dresser top and then angled the matching ivory jewelry case her grandmother had given her for her seventh birthday just so. She picked up her hair barrettes—first the ruby-studded butterfly clips, then the tortoise shell combs, and then a dozen more in every color of the rainbow—and laid them out in neat rows, spacing them evenly apart across the top of the bureau.

"Anya will arrange those for you in the morning," Jacob Kessler said, knocking softly on her door.

Hannah looked up at her father through the mirror. Standing there in his thick, dark purple robe, his full head of white hair combed back, still slick from his evening bath, he seemed, for the first time to her, to be getting old, and it sent a chill down her spine.

"That's alright," she said softly. "I need to do these things myself."

"I know this seems difficult now, Channeleh, but, in the end, you'll see, it's the right thing."

Hannah stopped rearranging and moved to the window, her back toward her father as she looked out across the whole of Prague glittering in the clear night sky.

"You're too young, you can't see the big picture. At your age, no one can," Jacob Kessler said in a warm voice.

"Didn't you ever have a dream, Papa?" she asked without turning around. "Something that lived inside you so strongly that it could not—would not—be denied. Something so powerful it consumes you night and day?"

Jacob Kessler walked across the room and gently put his hands on his daughter's shoulders. "Of course, I did," he said with a sigh. "I was going to be an admiral in the royal navy, with an entire fleet, more than a thousand ships, under my command."

"So why didn't you do it?" she asked, turning slightly toward him.

"Why? Because your grandfather forbid it, that's why. Because I had responsibilities and obligations, to the family, to the business. And, most of all because... it's no place for a Jew. The Tsar would never allow such a thing. It's a very complicated world, Channelah. It's going to be tough enough for you as it is just being a woman. Being Jewish only makes it that much harder, I'm afraid."

"It doesn't seem like it matters at all. You're not only accepted, but you're one of the most respected members of the community. I see the way people act when they're around you."

"Ah yes," Jacob Kessler said with a smile. "But do you see how they act when they're not around us? That's a different story altogether. It's not that we're not accepted, we are. But only so far. If there is one thing history has taught us over and over, it's that we are never really completely accepted. Look, it's the twentieth century and still there are pogroms every week throughout Poland and Russia with hundreds of Jews being beaten and robbed. And why? Just because they are Jews, no other reason. We may be tolerated, yes; even embraced by that small minority with some principles and a kind heart, God bless them everyone; but never, it seems, are we truly accepted."

"Will that ever change, Papa?"

"Maybe if we have a homeland again. But even then I'm not so sure. Maybe if the Holy Land is given back to the Jews as the Almighty decreed to Moses so many thousands of years ago. Maybe then. That's why the Zionists have been making so much noise about a Jewish state for the last thirty or forty years. Without a country, we are nothing, just a bunch of nomads eternally getting kicked about from one end of Creation to the other. No, Channelah, without a place to call our own, we may never find acceptance anywhere."

Jacob Kessler, turned away from his daughter, walked over to the dresser, and picked up the portrait of his wife from where it sat, shining in the moonlight. "God, I miss you," Jacob said touching his lips softly to the glass in the picture.

"No, Channelah. They are called dreams for a reason," Jacob sighed, picking out a flower from the vase and twirling it back and forth between his thumb and his forefinger. "Because…they aren't real. Besides, you'll have a nice garden at the summerhouse you and Friedrich will buy at the Black Sea. You can enjoy your flowers there," he said calmly.

'*You and Friedrich.*' He said it just like that Hannah thought. No hesitation, no difficulty putting those words together. To her father, it came as naturally as if he had been buttering bread.

Jacob Kessler kissed his daughter's forehead gently. "Good night," he said, "sleep tight." Then he pulled the door shut behind him. Tears welling up in her eyes, Hannah picked up her mother's picture and began to cry. "What am I going to do, mama? What am I going to do?" she sobbed. Then, Hannah threw herself on her bed and cried herself to sleep.

. . . .

Twenty-three

The insurance institute, four stories of flat, gray blocks held together by mortar even grayer still, was every bit as drab and uninviting as Hannah imagined it would be. What she hadn't foreseen were her fellow students, each more pale than the one before and an instructor so colorless as to seem almost transparent. "Miss Kessler? Miss Kessler?" the teacher, Victor Karpacz, asked a disaffected Hannah as she sat staring out one of the windows from her seat at the back of the room.

"Forty-two," Hannah snapped.

"Forty-two what?"

"Uhhh…" she stuttered, beginning to turn red.

"The answer is amortization," Karpacz said shaking his head. "We were discussing the theorem behind the actuarial tables. We finished our equations five minutes ago. Please pay attention, Miss Kessler," Victor Karpacz pleaded, the veins on his bald scalp twitching. "We're two weeks into the semester. Your papa will think we're not doing our jobs here and he'll withdraw his annual grant and we'll all be out of luck."

"I'm sorry," Hannah said quietly.

A moment later, the school bell rang and the class began shuffling about, gathering up their books and papers.

"Tonight, read chapter two," Karpacz instructed. "Answer the even-numbered problems at the end. And ten bonus points for anyone who solves number fifty-one." The assignment evoked a collective sigh from the students and they trailed out one by one, leaving only Hannah and the pale, old instructor.

With his hollow cheeks, bottomless black eyes, and a patchy tuft of white hair circling his bald pate, Victor Karpacz looked more than a little like a ghost. His frame was thin and bony and his Adam's apple stuck out so far most people thought it would burst out of his throat whenever he laughed or coughed.

"I know this isn't the most fascinating material for you, Miss Kessler" Karpacz said frankly. "At your age, I can't say I was much different. But it's important work to many people."

"And completely unimportant to others," she lamented.

"Nevertheless. You are here and I am here and we have to make the best of it. And I think, that if you give it some time, you'll see. It's not so horrible after all. Maybe not great, but not as bad as you think, either. Besides, it's what Herr Kessler wants, isn't it?"

Karpacz had begun to convince Hannah, even uplift her for a moment—until he played that last card, her father.

"My father—" Hannah began, then thinking better of it, held her tongue. "Good night, Herr Karpacz. I'll see you Monday," she said and gathered up her books and bag and headed for the door.

"Actually, you'll see me tomorrow night. I've been invited to attend the banquet as one of your father's guests. So you see, I was serious when I said he will think I'm not doing my job. How can I sit there through the appetizer and the soup and the entrees and the dessert and the port afterward if you haven't made even the slightest progress we can discuss? It can't be done. So, please, sometime between now and the hors d'oeurvres tomorrow evening, if you wouldn't mind cracking open the book to soak in even a few key phrases, I'd be much obliged. Good evening, and a pleasant Sabbath to you and your father, Miss Kessler," Victor Karpacz said. Then he grabbed his coat and hat and left, leaving Hannah alone with nothing but the blackboard and the long, dry calculations he scribbled there earlier that afternoon fading in the pale afternoon light as it filtered through the sooty windows.

. . . .

Twenty-four

In exchange for mucking out the stables below him, Marc Chagall took a loft, to sleep, to paint, to do whatever he wished—"so long as it would not embarrass the master of the house and was within the limits of the law," the groundskeeper had told him. It was a sweet arrangement for both parties, he thought. For a mere pittance in labor, situated as it was on a small hill along the eastern banks of the Vltava river, in one of the city's oldest and most well-to-do neighborhoods, the room's two western-facing windows opened out onto the whole of Prague below. And the tenants—no matter their financial status—enjoyed one of the finest views in the city as the sun worked its spectacular magic every evening at dusk over the river, the castle, and the spires of St. Vitus. But it was that very same fortuitous location—directly above the stalls requiring attention—that ensured the landlord that everyone who called this place home did at least what was expected of them per the agreement and usually, quite a bit more.

"Hey, Dedo, old pal," Chagall told the painter who sublet the loft from him three days a week, "Can't you smell that?" When an answer wasn't forthcoming, he spoke up a little louder. "Hey, Modigiliani, go earn some more of your rent, will you?"

"What?"

"Take a whiff, that's what."

"Oh. Okay, okay," Amedeo Modligliani said, putting his brush down as the church bell rang out four times.

"It's four o'clock already? I got practically nothing done today," Chagall said setting his brush and palette down. "I haven't even looked at the morning paper," he said picking it up and heading over to the window. He straddled one leg outside the sill and the other on the floor for balance. "Holy cow," he read somberly as he leaned against the window frame. "Tolstoy Dead."

"Rest his soul," Dedo said quietly. "What happened?"

"The eighty-two-year-old author of *War and Peace* and *Anna Karenina* succumbed to pneumonia aboard a train en route from his home in Moscow to Shamordino, his sister Marya's estate. He succumbed at one a.m in the station master's house in Kozyolsk where he had taken shelter for the night. Hey, I was just there on the train, a few days ago."

"I loved *Anna Karenina*."

"Incredible," Chagall said continuing to scan the paper. "There was another pogrom in Kiev last week. Twenty-two people dead, almost sixty hospitalized.

"A pogrom, what's that, like a tornado or something?"

"Sort of," Chagall said. "A bunch of crazies come through town and kills as many Jews as they find and destroy as much property as they can. It's kind of like a human tornado."

"What?! Why on earth would anybody do that?"

"They're afraid. Afraid of things—and people—they don't understand."

"I'm scared of things too, but I don't go around murdering innocent people because of it."

"This is nothing new, Dedo. This has been going on in my neighborhood for hundreds of years." He scanned the rest of the paper, then put it down, and stared out the window. After a minute something caught his eye. "Oh my," Chagall purred. "Oh my, my, my, my."

"What now?" the Italian asked, continuing to apply paint to canvas in short, quick strokes.

"Dedo, my friend, is there anything more amazing than the female of the species?"

"No argument there."

"We are the same species exactly, yet it is as if we are completely different creatures. We are always pushing against the elements, trying to advance ourselves in some small, but crude, way. But they, they seem to flow with life, to be a part of it, one with it. We're warriors and hunters. They... they are so much more...evolved. Sometimes it seems as if we are holding them back as a species. And some of them... the more magnificent among them...they can do something nothing else can—they can make you forget time exists."

"Hey," Dedo said finally, putting down his brush and palette. "What are you looking at, anyway?"

"What is the sexiest thing you can imagine?" Chagall taunted.

"You'll have to make these questions a little harder," Dedo said, wiping his hands clean skipping toward the window Chagall was straddling. "A woman getting undressed, of course."

"Absolutely... wrong," Chagall said with a sly grin as he continued staring out the window. "Poor Dedo," he shook his head with a sly grin. "Poor, poor Dedo. Sure, undressing is nice, but it's precisely the opposite, watching them get dressed—especially when they don't know they're being watched—that's the best," he told his friend and pointed him toward a window across the street from them. "They're like tigresses in the jungle, powerful, and constantly preening and primping. First they pick out their finery, you know, something to wear underneath. Delicacy by delicacy they position everything just so," he said, his hands tracing his waist. "Then below, they slide themselves into their lace like a rose laid into a silk vase," he continued mimicking. "Then the stockings. They go through their drawers, looking for just the right pair, checking this one and that for runs and holes. Was there ever a more sensual garment invented than stockings, Dedo? I shouldn't imagine so. If I ever come across the man who invented these silken sheaths, I will kiss him, they are amazing. Then, they're off to the closet. A dress? A skirt? Blouse? Sweater? Flowers, prints, dark, light. You can see how their magnificent feminine minds are working. It's so sexy watching them go through the process. Picking up this garment and discarding that one. Then picking it back up again and matching it top against bottom, top against hair, bottom to shoes, the black pair, then the brown, then black but a higher heel," he said flexing his imaginary pumps. "Then, they stop. It's time to stop for the makeup. They sit down at their tables and mirrors and begin to paint. And what artists they are, everyone one of them. Far better than you or I. Instinctively they know exactly which colors are right for them that day and which are not. They powder and they blush, highlighting here, and plucking there. First they soften the lines," he said. "Then the eyes. Do you see how much time they spend on the eyes? The shadowing and the colors and the lashes like butterfly wings. Wonderful, just wonderful. And ah, the lipstick. Is there anything better than watching a woman trace her soft pink lips with color, pouting and pursing them just so? Then the hair, brushing it until it shines and then deciding whether to put it up and reveal the soft, pale white of their necks or drop it down to sway and tantalize us. Then they slip into the clothes and then the jewelry. Just the right amount. They know Dedo. They know just how much draws you in with its glitter and how much distracts from their own gems, their eyes, their lips, their luxurious smiles. Then, just before they set out, the perfume—the flavoring, the spice. A dash of sweet, fragrant scent here, a dab there, to lure you from a distance, so subtly you don't even know you're being pursued. I tell you, it's a miracle, almost like watching fruit ripen before your eyes," Marc Chagall said, his eyes wide with pleasure, his lips smacking quietly. "There is nothing better. And who do they do all this for? For us, Dedo. They do all this for us. Each with their own personal, fantastic style. Oh no. The burlesque houses have it absolutely wrong. The putting-on is *much* sexier than the taking off," Chagall said, finishing in a whisper and walking away from the window.

"You're crazy," Modigiliani laughed, then put down his palette and brushes. "Whoever heard of a man asking a woman to put on her clothes?"

"That's the difference between you and me, Dedo."

"Just me? Oh no, my friend, that's the difference between you and every other man on the planet," he answered as he stripped out of his painters' rags.

"So be it," Chagall said with a warm smile. "Hey, where do you think you're going? Saturday night is your turn to make dinner."

"Not this Saturday night, *paisano*. I've got to earn my share of the rent somehow. I'm waiting tables at some big to-do in one of those castles on the other side of town. But hey, come with

162

me, I'll get you plenty to eat out the back door. Besides, whatever I throw your way from there is bound to be ten times better than anything we can pull together here.

"I don't know, I've got stuff to finish up here."

"You're losing the light anyway. Plus, there'll be plenty of women there just the way you like them—fully clothed!" Dedo Modigliani teased with a laugh.

. . . .

Twenty-five

Hannah Kessler sat curled up, one leg tucked up beneath her on the cushion of the swinging, wicker loveseat in the sunroom of her father's Prague townhouse, the other leg rocked her gently back and forth. The last rays of sunshine beaming down on her, she sat facing the garden, a thick, green book in her hands as she boned up on the soil preferences of *tulipa suaveolens*, the Van Thol tulip, renowned for its bold fragrances.

"I hope you're at least brushing up on something important, like the proper negligence clauses to include in commercial liability policies," Jacob Kessler said as he entered the sunroom in his dress shirt, tie in hand. "Oy, Channelah," he said tipping up the book to read the title. "No more flowers, please. We've got to be at the banquet in less than an hour. Please go get dressed."

"But, Papa—"

"No buts. We agreed. Business first, flowers after," he said, putting his hand out for the textbook.

"This isn't business. It's a bunch of stuffy, old men and their even stuffier old wives…"

"This isn't business? What is it, then? Pleasure?" Jacob Kessler asked. "These events are where the real business gets done. Not in some office. That's the first lesson Victor Karpacz should be teaching you. The insurance business isn't about policies or premiums, it's not about actuarial tables. That's technical nonsense. Anyone can do the sums. The heart of this business—any business—is the relationship between client and provider. And when a client—your biggest client, mind you—invites you to his favorite charity's fundraising dinner, you go to his fundraising dinner and you fund. Right?" he asked. "Right," he answered himself. "Thank you," he said, when she closed the book, handed it to him, and headed for the stairs.

Jacob Kessler stood outside his daughter's half-open bedroom door and watched quietly for a moment as Hannah brushed her hair in the mirror at her vanity table, then he knocked gently. When she looked up in the mirror, he didn't say a word, he just held out the limp ribbon of silk that was his bowtie in his hand.

"Come on," she relented, smiling in the mirror.

"These things just aren't the same without your mother," Jacob said sitting down on the stool next to Hannah and picking up the photo of his wife. "She was the center of attention at these things. It didn't matter who was there. Kings, queens, ambassadors, judges, everyone wanted to be with Libby Kessler. She knew how to put people at ease and she was the life of any party. When she was with you, you felt like you were the only two people in the world. Do you think all these big shots came to see me? I was just an excuse for them to be near her, to bask inside her special glow, if only for a few hours. There was no one—no one—like your mother."

Putting the final touches on his tie, Hannah leaned down and put her face next to his. Reaching down, she took Jacob

Kessler's hand in hers, pressed it close against her cheek and kissed it. "I miss her too, Papa," she whispered.

"Do you know what her secret was? Fashion. Your mother could tell about people by the clothes they wore. She knew what interested them, what was important in their lives, what to say that was just right, literally, by the cloth they were cut from. She knew people. And she could always tell the bad insurance risks from the good ones by the way they dressed. Were their socks always loose around their ankles and they were careless? Was their tie always straight as an arrow or crooked like the person wearing it? She was the supreme underwriter in the family, your mother," Jacob Kessler said, a warm smile on his face.

The Sternbersky Palace lit up the crisp, dark, night sky as the Banker's Ball got underway. By the time Chagall and Dedo arrived, the endless procession of gilded carriages had already begun dropping off Bohemia's crème de la crème all decked out in their finery at the front gates and they could her the orchestra playing a waltz inside.

"Wow," Chagall said, walking past the crowd. "Do you see the jewelry on those women? The necklaces alone are worth more than the entire population of Vitebsk."

"Come on, I'm already late," Dedo scolded. Chagall started to move, then Dedo said, "Not that way. We go in the back," and they turned around and headed for the servant's entrance.

Chagall stood behind Dedo Modigliani at the back door to the kitchen for a moment and soaked in the scene inside the bowels of Count Sternbersky's "little town house" as it was known in certain circles.

"Hot soup. Coming through," a tuxedoed waiter shouted as he weaved through the palace's crowded kitchen balancing a tray full of soup bowls in the palm of one hand high above his head and a steaming loaf of crusty bread in a white-linen lined basket in the other. A dozen giant pots watched by as many chefs burbled on the left. On the right half a dozen bakers kneaded dough. In the center of the room a dozen cooks sliced and diced vegetables while a line of sauté cooks shook their copper frying pans vigorously back and forth to the oil-flamed sizzles along the back wall. In between, a herd of waiters scurried around, filling their trays with rolls and salads and appetizers of every sort as they glided through the steam and mist and then out to the grand ballroom through a set of double swinging doors at the far end of the kitchen.

"Stay here and stay out of the way while I check in and change," Dedo instructed him. "I'll bring you something back in a few minutes. Do not move. Is that clear? Do *not* move."

Chagall grinned weakly. Then, as soon as his friend was out of sight he said to himself, "Sorry, Dedo, old pal, but I'm not getting this close to those patrons of the arts without at least taking a whiff of what all that money smells like." Then he moved toward the far end of the kitchen and took up a position near the dry goods pantry, a clear view into the ballroom through the two sets of swinging doors. From there he moved into the small corridor separating the first set of doors from the kitchen to the second that opened into ballroom, and shielded the guests from the culinary commotion necessary to create such an event. Chagall observed the rhythm, and then—as though it were his official duty—took up a post at the ballroom door, opening it for the waiters to pass, shutting it behind them, and taking every opportunity in between to scan the party floor.

"Smile," Chagall instructed the first waiter who whizzed by him. "Happy, happy!" he told the next one, he told the next, waving his arms in a big circle in front of him. "Wait," he told the third, then straightened the young man's bow tie, grabbed an hors d'oeuvre from his tray, and sent him on his way.

With a break in the traffic, Marc Chagall held the door open and took his first good look at the palatial late seventeenth century ballroom. "Holy Moses," he whispered to himself, as he soaked in the masterworks adorning the twenty-foot high walls. "There must be a million rubles worth of art out there."

"Ten million rubles worth," a waiter smart-alecked as he sped past the awestruck artist. "And that's just at table number twelve."

The server was right. There before his very eyes, sat perhaps one-third of the aggregated wealth of central Europe. And, he realized a moment later, at the most prominent table in the center of the room, next to her father, sat Hannah Kessler. "It's her," Chagall whispered to himself, his eyes lighting up instantly, his lips curling into a wide smile. Moving out of the way, he stood to one side of the swinging doors and focused on Hannah.

"There you are," a tuxedoed Dedo, balancing a tray full of bread rolls said, startling him. "*Jesus Christos*, I've been looking all over for you. I gave up. You can't stay here, come on back inside."

"She's here," Chagall said ignoring him completely.

"You can't be here. I told you to stay by the back door. If you get caught, I'll lose my job."

"Forget your job. This is about *love*," he said, his eyes on fire now.

"Huh?" Dedo asked, confused.

"It's *her*, the girl I told you about."

"Which girl, the one getting dressed? I told you, they're all dressed here, let's go," he said, trying to turn Chagall back around by the elbow.

"No, the girl from the train. Hannah. Give me your uniform," Chagall demanded, his eyes locked onto Hannah.

"What?"

"Take off your clothes. I need to get out there and talk to her. Hurry up," Chagall said, kicking off his shoes and unbuttoning his shirt.

"Have you lost your mind?"

"Definitely. And my heart too. Strip, and make it fast."

"What are you going to do?"

"I'm going to talk to her."

"We're not allowed to speak to the guests unless spoken to."

"Then, give me your pencil and paper," he said grabbing them from Dedo, then scribbling furiously on the page. "Ok, I won't say a word," he said handing the pencil back.

Dedo looked in his friend's eyes and could see it was hopeless. "Alright," he finally relented and handed Chagall the tray then starting disrobing. "Just don't make a scene. That's all I ask."

"Relax."

"Relax? Are you insane? I'm standing here half naked in the entry way to the grand ballroom at Sternbersky Palace and you're about to go out there and impersonate me in front of some of the most important people in Europe, people who might someday buy my work—or yours! And over what? Over some girl you met on a train and I'm supposed to relax?"

"This isn't just about some girl," he said, quickly making the final adjustments to the uniform. "I told you, this is about love. Love, Dedo, true love. The core of everything that is. I ask you, without love, is there life?" Chagall said laughing and taking the tray from his friend. Then he shoved a roll in his friend's mouth and stepped out into the crowded ballroom.

Dedo pulled the bread from his mouth and whispered in a loud voice to his friend, "Remember, serve from the right. From the *right*," he emphasized, whisking his arm back and forth.

Chagall worked his way from table to table, setting down a basket of rolls at each one, moving ever closer toward the center table. When he reached it however, he paused, put his head down, removed the tongs from the basket, and began placing the rolls, one by one on each guest's bread dish, starting at the far end from his target and circling ever closer to Hannah.

"So, Zack. Do you think Brodsky will go for it?" he heard Jacob Kessler ask the man seated across from him.

"If the terms are right, I don't see why not," Zack answered, sounding every bit the banker he was. "What do you

170

think, Baron?" he asked the man to his right, Gunzberg, the international financier.

"It's a growing market, I agree, but how are they going to get the sugar there?"

"There are no rail lines between Russia and the United States," Samuel Poliakiv, the railroad magnate pointed out. "And for good reason, that's very hostile terrain, across Siberia, into Alaska, and down into Canada. Not even the Chinese will go in there and lay track. And those brave rascals will go almost anywhere and do just about anything."

"I think they plan to ship it from the port at Anadyi straight into San Francisco Harbor," Max Breslow informed the group.

"In that case, if they can still offer a competitively priced product, yes," Poliakiv said, "Brodsky might be willing."

"Send me the proposal," Abe Zack said. "I'll see that Brodsky reads it."

As he reached Hannah, he took a moment to close his eyes and take a deep breath of her sweet scent before setting her roll down on its dish. Before he could finish drawing her in, a loud voice startled him. "So, Mr. Chagall, how are tips these days?"

"Ex-, excuse me?" he asked, his head pulled in like a turtle's now.

"How are tips?" Friedrich Kohlman, Jr. asked again. "In the table-waiting business, you know, as opposed to say… the art business. That is you, under there, isn't it Mr. Chagall?"

"Yes. Tips are fine, thank you," Chagall said. He looked up and nervously over his shoulder across the room at Dedo who cringed as he watched the proceedings fitfully from just inside the kitchen doorway.

"Papa, you remember Mr. Chagall, don't you?"

"No, I can't say that I do," Jacob Kessler said, annoyed.

"The artist we met coming here on the train to Prague?" Hannah reminded him.

"Yes, of course," Jacob said drolly.

"So, you're an artist?" Samuel Poliakiv asked.

"A very talented one," Hannah explained. "I saw his work coming over on the train from Moscow."

"Might I have seen your work anywhere?" Poliakiv continued.

"You've heard of the Hermitage?"

"Of course," the financier said stoutly. "You were exhibited at the Hermitage?"

"Actually, it was across the street," he said with a smile. "That is, until the police told me to pack up and move," Chagall said with a laugh. "No, sir. I'm still trying to make a name for myself. But I'll get there."

"Good for you lad," Abe Zack commended him.

"There aren't enough young people like that in the world today, are there Jacob?" Gunzberg asked. "People with confidence in themselves who will do whatever it takes—waiting tables, even—to get where they want to go."

"Well, sir," Chagall explained, "I just believe that a man's got to make his own way in the world," he said casting an eye toward Friedrich, Jr.

"Here, here," Poliakiv agreed. "That deserves a toast," he said raising his glass. "Here's to making your own way."

172

"To making your own way," they all toasted.

"You must show us your work some day," Samuel Poliakiv said.

"Thank you, sir. Some day I will," Chagall said, then turned to Hannah. "And thank you, Miss," he said, pressing his note into her palm, startling her for a moment.

As he walked backed toward the kitchen, he stopped and turned back to see if Hannah had read his note.

Hannah waited until everyone's attention was focused on her father, who was about give a second toast, then she unfolded the note and read it: *Think free! Meet me at the tower gate at midnight.*

She looked up just in time to see him turn back once more before he went into the kitchen and smiled, at which he leapt into the air, nearly knocking over a waiter carrying a tray full of salads.

"I wasn't sure you'd come," Chagall said, looking up at the clock tower as the bells struck a quarter past midnight.

"Between Papa, Uncle Harry, and that awful Friedrich, Jr. watching over me every minute, it wasn't easy getting away. I finally had to tell them I wasn't feeling well. By the time I convinced them that I would be okay making my own way home... well, no matter. I'm here now," Hannah Kessler said with a warm smile.

"Indeed you are," Chagall said, beaming as she positively glistened in the moonlight. "How'd you like to come to a real party with me? I don't know if you're dressed properly for it," he said, taking a step a back and assessing her, "but I think we can fix you up a little."

"Fix me up a little?" she huffed. "This dress alone cost three hundred rubles. And the shoes, a hundred fifty more."

"Try not to mention that once we get there," he said, taking her arm and tucking it into his own. "This is a real party. You know someplace where people try to forget all their troubles and really let their hair down. If these folks thought somebody could afford nearly five hundred rubles just for some party clothes, there's no way they could forget their troubles. Come on," he said as they walked away from the castle.

As they left Marc Chagall and Hannah Kessler heard an awful screeching come from behind them. That was followed by some screams, the whinnying of a dozen or more horses, and the sounds of utter chaos. They turned just in time to see an automobile racing out of control and barreling toward them, its driver panic-stricken and flustered as he grasped at the steering wheel that had come off in his hands. Marc pulled Hannah out of the way as the vehicle passed them and they watched it crash into a large shed half a block away, which, judging by all the feathers flying and poultry fluttering about, was the palace's hen house.

Chagall left Hannah behind and ran to check on the driver. By the time, he had cleared the fallen planks and jumbles of hay, Hannah had caught up and the artist realized who was behind the wheel. "Oh, hey there, Friedrich," he said, extending his hand to help him out of the mess. "How are things in the automobile business these days? You know, as opposed to say, the coal mining business?"

"Very funny," Friedrich, Jr. said, refusing the hand and extricating himself from the car. Then he dusted off the feathers and broken eggs dripping from his hair, face, and tuxedo. When he had gotten most of the mess off, he turned to Hannah and said, "I thought you were sick and going home. I offered you a ride."

"Yes, and we can see what a good idea that would have been. It's a good thing Mr. Chagall came along when he did and offered to walk me home. Good night, Friedrich," Hannah said, tucking her arm back into Chagall's and walking out of the hen house.

"Yes, good night, Friedrich," Chagall said. "If I were you I don't know if I'd report this to my insurance company," he said as they left, laughing.

"I'm such an idiot," Chagall said kicking the ground and raising up a cloud of dirt as they walked along in the moonlight. "'*You must show us your work someday*,' he says. 'Someday, I will,' I say. What someday? There was my opportunity, maybe my only opportunity ever, to have someone as influential as that look at my work. I should have said, 'Yes, sir, how about tomorrow afternoon around four-thirty?' I'm so stupid. Stupid, stupid, stupid."

"Oh, I don't know," Hannah said, trying to comfort him. "For somebody who, as you put it, "travels in all the wrong circles," your poor circles seem to intersect with the rich ones often enough. I think you'll run into Poliakiv again or someone like him.

Besides," she said, clutching his arm more closely, "you've got me now. When you're ready to make a real showing of your work, I'll help you," she smiled warmly.

Soon enough, they came to a small hall sandwiched in between the row houses, its windows brightly lit up from the inside and its walls shaking from the music spilling out into the streets. Chagall led Hannah to a side window, put his hands around her waist and lifted her up so she could peek inside.

Hannah scanned the room through the tiny window. At the front of the dance hall on a small makeshift stage she watched as a dozen musicians played their instruments—fiddles, clarinets, flutes, cellos, and horns—in the most lively, bittersweet music she had ever heard.

"They're called *klezmorim*," Chagall explained. "It's from the Hebrew, *klezmer*. It means musical instruments. Every member of a klezmer band is from one, large family and the songs they play have been in their family for generations." Taking her hand, he led her inside.

Marc Chagall grabbed a pair of drinks from the serving table near the door and handed one to Hannah. As they pulsed to the beat of the music he moved them toward the dance floor. As they neared the middle, Chagall threw his drink back in a single swig, then watched as Hannah did likewise. They set their glasses down on a ringside table and the artist took Hannah in his arms and waltzed her onto the dance floor and she laughed, and laughed, and laughed. She delighted in every twist and turn as Chagall twirled her around and, as graceful as she was, it was as though she fairly floated on air.

When the tune ended, the crowd applauded and then stopped to catch their breath. But before they could do so, the band struck up again, with an even livelier tune this time. A circle formed around the dance floor. The crowd began to clap in unison and in an instant, a pair of young bucks took center stage doing the kisotsky, springing up and down like grasshoppers, feet flying out and back, as the dance and its triple-time rhythm demanded. With the crowd cheering them on, the men challenged each other with one feat after another designed to flaunt their strength, agility, and flexibility. As the beat changed, they took their bows to a standing ovation, then moved off the dance floor and melted back into the crowd.

Chagall grabbed Hannah and pulled her toward the floor. "Come on, let's kisotsky," he said.

"I don't know how," she resisted, but only for a minute, laughing and protesting. Then, grabbing a shot glass from a neighbor in the crowd, she guzzled it down and joined Chagall on the floor.

"Like this," he showed her, folding his arms into each other and demonstrating how the folk dance worked. Down, out, up, out, and so on.

Hannah followed suit and within a minute danced as though she had done this her whole life.

"That's it," he shouted as the pace picked up and he danced lower and lower, with Hannah following along, move for move. As the music came to a frenzied head, he yelled, "Think free!" And so Hannah did and they lost themselves in the music and the joy and the raw energy of life, not a care in the world.

When the beat changed again, Hannah and Chagall stepped aside and fell into each other's arms. They stood and clapped and cheered along with everyone else as a new pair of dancers, two burly men with long black beards took the dance floor. They challenged each other as they bobbed up and down, reaching into the crowd and each grabbing a small child and the chair they sat in, lifting it above their heads from a single chair leg. From children, they moved onto women, and ultimately, to full grown men, until they each tumbled backward into the crowd laughing and cheering.

"You think that's so strong?" Hannah challenged the crowd, kicking off her shoes and slipping off her knee-high stockings. Then she stood up, wriggled her pink, pedicured toes on the floor, unhooked her skirt, and threw it on a chair. Standing there in her frilly bloomers, Hannah Kessler screwed her courage together and marched over to a half wall that stood about waist high and a few inches wide, dividing one corner of the room for about twenty feet. "Watch this," she said.

Then in a single move, Hannah flipped herself head over heels and catapulted onto the slender top beam of the wall, landing on one hand, her arm fully extended, her body perfectly straight and balanced, her toes in pointed, perfect alignment, not a millimeter of sway in her form whatsoever.

From there, Hannah flipped and twisted across the narrow beam as though it were the broadest boulevard. Her taut, young body was fluid and strong, and her contortions so smooth and graceful it seemed as though she were uninhibited by such things as a spine or gravity. The crowd watched her every move in awe until finally, holding herself perfectly still, she focused her

178

concentration and then, in a flurry of twists and turns across the beam, she leaped into the air, tumbling twice in midair and landing perfectly in front of Chagall, where she grinned gleefully, took her bows as the audience applauded wildly, and—the alcohol finally catching up with her—fainted in a dizzying spin into the young artist's waiting arms.

. . . .

Twenty-six

"Sometimes, being a man's not all it's cracked up to be, is it?" Chagall asked, as he held Hannah, hunched over on her knees, one arm around her waist, the other hand holding her forehead. She released one final, steamy, gut-wrenching heave into the swift-moving waters of the river in front of her, then Marc Chagall pulled her back up slowly and let her collapse into his lap.

"Oh my god," she groaned, holding her stomach. "I don't know how you guys do it."

"Shhh," he whispered, gently tilting her back in his arms. He pulled a handkerchief from his pocket and dabbed her face clean with it. "Just rest." He cradled her there and watched as little wisps of steam curled out of her tender, pink nostrils, her eyes closed, her small, delicate hands wrapped around his.

After a while, her eyes still closed, Hannah turned toward him and, in a soft voice asked, "Why do you want to paint?"

"It's not a question of wanting to or not wanting to. For me, painting is like breathing, it's something I have to do. I don't know," he mused. "I just see so much beauty and love in the world. And yet so much pain. I feel like if I can show people enough of the love through my painting, maybe somehow the suffering will diminish. I know it sounds silly, but it's how I feel."

"Tell me about Paris. Tell me everything," she said, the moonbeams glistening in her hair.

"Paris," Chagall said, savoring even the name. "Paris is amazing. There can't have ever been a city in any other time or any other place as incredible as Paris—not for artists anyway. Not for free thinkers, not for philosophers, for lovers of life... or just for... lovers," he purred unctuously.

Hannah smiled and turned her head away so he wouldn't see her blush. "What about the gardens? I've heard the gardens are magnificent."

"They are," he said. I don't think I've ever seen anything as spectacular as the *Jardins des Tuilieries*."

"I thought you hadn't ever been there?" Hannah asked.

"I haven't. I've only seen it in books and postcards," he said excitedly. "When you first walk in there are a dozen rows of violets. Behind those there are three layers of hydrangeas, a kind of a lavender, then a white, and then a deep blue. Then there are the rose gardens, and the tulip fields, and the lilies, and daffodils," he continued, his eyes closed, inhaling as though he could actually smell the blossoms in front of him. And as he went on describing the blooms, a small smile curled up in the corner of Hannah's lips as she imagined him there capturing a glorious Parisian spring day on the canvas poised in front of him.

"That's brilliant, positively brilliant," she said, her eyes open now. "I never would have thought to set off the lilies against each other like that. But I'm not so sure I like what they've done with the roses," she went on excitedly. "I've got to get there," she said getting up.

"Hey," Chagall said trying to stop her. "What are you doing?"

"Whoa," she said losing her balance and reaching out to grab him.

"You can't just get up like that," he chided, taking her arm and steadying her.

"Whew," she sighed, regaining her balance.

"You're going to have to take it easy for a bit. And, tomorrow morning, you'll wish you had jumped off that train because that would've been gentle compared to the way you're going to feel. Come on," he said, putting his arm in hers and starting to slowly walk with her. "Nice and easy, that's it. Good…"

They continued along the riverbank arm in arm, contented in the moment until they came to a small wall.

"Oh my," Hannah said peeking over it. "What's that?"

"That's the Old Jewish Cemetery," Chagall explained. "It's one of the most famous places in Prague. It dates back to the fifteenth century."

"Why are all the tombstones like that, all bunched up and jumbled around?"

"Come on," he said hopping over the wall and reaching back across for her. "I'll show you."

She climbed over and took his hand as they walked among the gravestones jutting up from every angle as if they were washed ashore in a storm and filling the grounds from end to end. "There are so many of them."

"Twelve thousand graves for sure. Some say as many as a hundred thousand more buried below."

"Below?"

"This is Josefov, the old Jewish district in Prague," he said pointing at the surrounding neighborhood. "The wall went up around the ghetto in 1254 to make sure people complied with the church laws forbidding Jews to live interspersed with Catholics. Why? Because the Jews were different from them. They had skills and they were educated. They could read and write and it scared those who couldn't. And so, if they could only live in this one part of town, then they could also only die in this one part of town and be buried in this one cemetery. When they ran out of room, they moved a layer of dirt on top of the ground to make space for more people to be buried. And so it went, year after year, decade after decade until the emperor, Joseph II, abolished the residency restrictions in 1784. For more than 500 years the Jews of Prague were restricted to this tiny little section of town. Still, this became a renowned center for learning. That's the Old-New Synagogue. It was built in the middle of the thirteenth century. That's the Klausen Synagogue, over there," he said pointing to a building in the far corner of the cemetery. "Mordechai Maisel who was the head of the Jewish community built it in honor of a visit to the ghetto from the Emperor Maximillian II in 1573. Over there," he said, pointing to the opposite side of the field, "that's the Pinkasova Synagogue, built in 1535. They continued walking among the stones until Chagall stopped suddenly. "And this," he said, pointing at the large, intricately carved tombstone in front of him with a lion's head at the top center and Hebrew writing covering nearly every other inch of the stone. "This is Rabbi Loew's grave. He's the golem rabbi. Do you know about the legend of the golem?"

"The what? No, what's that?"

"Sit," he said, setting her down against a stone.

"The legend goes something like this," he began, his eyes widening. "In the late sixteenth century here in Josefov, there lived a rabbi by the name of Rabbi Loew. He was a *tzaddik*, a very, very wise man. It troubled him to see his congregation have to work so hard for so little pay and to suffer so under the hands of their oppressors. Every day, it seemed there was some kind of trouble. Sometimes there were pogroms and lots of innocent people were beaten and their homes and their businesses destroyed by hooligans. In 1389 alone, three thousand people were killed in a single pogrom.

"If that weren't bad enough, sometimes, when a Christian baby died, they would take it into the ghetto and leave it in the gutter and then "find" it, claiming that some Jew had killed the baby in a kind of religious ritual murder. They would arrest the first person they saw, claim he was guilty, and immediately hang him in the town square. This went on for a long, long time until one day, the legend says, the Rabbi remembered something his father had told him as a child. He told him how to make a golem, a kind of robot."

"It looks like a human and it does human things, but it doesn't have a soul, so it's not human. Since a golem is not human it never gets tired and it doesn't need to eat or drink.

"So the rabbi got it into his head that he would make a golem. That golem would become his servant and help his congregation. The golem would help his congregants with their chores and at night, wearing an amulet with special powers the rabbi gave him, the golem would patrol the streets at night, invisible to everyone except the rabbi, and he would catch all the people trying to frame the Jews and he would tie them up, dead babies and all, and lead them to the sheriff's office.

"So, the rabbi and his son-in-law and his best pupils went to the river and took the wettest clay they could find and sculpted a figure of a man almost three and a half meters tall. They walked around the sculpture three times and said the special incantation. When they were done, the clay began to glow as if on fire," Chagall said nearly breathless.

"So they started around three times again, giving the next incantation as they did, and the golem began to cool off. When they went around again, the golem grew hair, and fingernails and toenails slid into place, and the golem stood up straight. 'Now listen to me, golem,' Rabbi Loew said. 'You will do as I say, when I say. You will not want from food or drink. You will not tire and nothing—neither sword, nor flame, nor any thing—shall be able to smite you. You shall do my people's bidding as I instruct.' And the golem nodded solemnly, because, without a soul, a golem cannot feel emotion. Well, in a matter of months the golem had exposed so many people intent on falsely accusing Jews that the rest of the citizens voted in a law making it illegal to falsely accuse Jews of ritual murder ever again."

"That's wonderful," Hannah said. "But what happened to the golem after he saved all the people?"

"Well, he saw all the people and their emotions and he became jealous and tried to mimic them and he became violent. So, the rabbi decided to relieve him of his life, which he did by reversing the prayers and returning the golem to dust."

"That's a great story," Hannah said. Then, realizing that she was squeezing Chagall's hands so tightly she had nearly cut off the circulation, she pulled away, blushing, and apologizing.

"Thank you," he said, shaking his hand to get the blood flowing again.

"I'm sorry," she laughed.

"I'll survive," Chagall said, taking her hand back gently. He looked into those eyes and lost himself deep inside her. Then Marc Chagall pulled her close and whispered, "Has anyone ever told you what an amazing woman you are? Simply amazing," he sighed. "I've never met anyone like you. When I'm with you, it's as if time doesn't exist." He drew in a deep breath, then stood up, and pulled her up along with him. "Let's get you home," he said quietly as they set out for her house, the dawn breaking just beyond the horizon.

"Home? Oh my god, Papa," Hannah said starting to run off. But Chagall took her arm and stopped her. "I've got to go," she said urgently.

"I know," he said. Then Marc Chagall took Hannah in his arms, pulled her close, and, pressing his lips against hers, kissed her until she was breathless. When he finally let her go, Hannah could barely stand and Marc Chagall felt as if he were lighter than air, floating above the ground.

Hannah pulled herself together and whispered, "I'd better be going."

"Can I see you again?" the artist asked, his pale blue eyes sparkling in the first ray of sunlight peeking over the horizon.

"You'd better," Hannah said laughing, then turned and ran home.

186

Expecting the worst, Hannah Kessler steeled herself when she heard her father come down the stairs toward the breakfast room on Sunday morning. She could always tell what kind of mood he was in by the way he descended the stairs. There was something in his gait, and each of his sentiments—cheer, boredom, weariness, anger—had its own tempo and tone. This morning, Jacob Kessler came down the stairs in short, harsh, deliberate steps. When he neglected to stop on the landing, sigh, and wind his pocket watch as he usually did, Hannah knew he was especially agitated. And so, she exchanged only a single, icy glance with him as he entered the room, then turned away, and gazed out the window into the small, common garden their townhouse shared with the other homes on the block. It had snowed sometime before dawn and the yard, the benches, bushes, trees, everything, lay there as if covered in a puffy, white blanket of snowy silence.

Pulling out his chair in one swift move, Jacob Kessler took his place at the head of the table. He was, as always on Sunday mornings, crisply but comfortably dressed in his pajamas, robe, and slippers, his thick hair neatly combed straight back in the same wave for over half a century now.

Hannah watched him out of the corner of her eye as he began his morning regimen. He twisted the lid off of the small china urn in front of him and took out a healthy pinch of the black tea leaves he ordered special from London four times a year. He filled the silver tea strainer to the brim, then tamped it down with his thumb, topping it off with one final pinch. Then he lifted the teapot lid, submerged the brew, and refit the lid, screwing it around three times exactly. He picked up the long, shiny knife from its place next to the bread tray where Beatrix, the housekeeper, always set it, and then Jacob Kessler mumbled the blessing over bread.

Hannah watched as he sliced off the heel of the loaf of challah and then three more thick pieces. Taking two pieces for himself, he pushed the bread dish away. Then crudely, he spread one pat of butter on the smaller slice, and two on the larger one, setting them down at right angles to each other along the edge of his breakfast dish.

Hearing a slight noise, Hannah turned and saw Beatrix peeking out through a crack in the swinging kitchen door. The maid waited until Jacob had set down his butter knife and poured himself a glass of water, her indication that it was time to serve the eggs and so, she shuffled in from the kitchen.

"*Gutten tag,*" the housekeeper barely whispered, having used her own barometer—Jacob Kessler's pinky finger— to gauge his mood that day. When he was relaxed it stood stylishly and delicately out from the fork. On mornings like this, when it was curled so tightly around the silverware that it was turning purple, she knew to spoon out the scrambled eggs and then make a hasty retreat to the kitchen.

As Hannah knew they would, they ate in near silence for nearly half an hour. The clinking and scraping of silverware on china the only sounds punctuating the air until Jacob Kessler crossed his knife and fork on the plate in front of him signifying he was finished. Then, reaching for the sugar bowl, he plucked a single cube from it, placed it in his mouth and, as his father before him and his father before that, bit down on it squarely between his upper and lower front teeth, poured a cup of steaming hot tea into his cup, and sipped it down in a single, slurping swig through the sugary cube until it had dissolved completely on his satisfied tongue.

"You don't have to talk to me," Hannah said, pulling the napkin from her lap and setting it on the table. "I said I was sorry, that's all I can do."

Jacob Kessler drew in his breath and looked as if he was about to speak, but he recoiled instead and, turning away from his daughter, just heaved a heavy sigh.

She watched for several minutes as her father stared coldly off into space, then Hannah stood up and crossed the room to leave. She walked past his stiff, silent frame, through the arch into the front hallway. As she began up the stairs, Jacob Kessler placed his napkin on the empty plate in front of him, pushed himself away from the table, and stood up. Hannah stopped and watched as he pushed in his chair and walked over to her, taking up a place one step below hers.

He moved in close to her and then said, "This is serious business we are here for. It's time for you to grow up and realize that." Then, Jacob Kessler put his head down and moved past her up the stairs and into his room, shutting the door behind him with a single, deliberate thud.

. . . .

Twenty-seven

"Manure, snow, it doesn't matter today Dedo. I could shovel the world and then go back and do it again," Chagall declared into bright, morning light. He tore into the six-foot high bank of white powder that had boxed them inside the barn, flinging bucket-sized lumps of snow left and right, and clearing a path like a polar bear through ice.

"Great," Dedo said eagerly putting his shovel down. "Let me know when you're done."

"And do you know why?" Chagall asked, still stoking away furiously. "Because I am in love, Dedo. This is the most incredible woman in the world. She is bright, and funny, and charming, and when I am with her time stands still. I cannot see anything but her. I cannot hear anything but her voice. I just look into those sparkling blue eyes and the way those pink lips spread so wide to reveal that big, glittering white smile of hers and I swear, it's as if I have wings. Forget hurricanes, forget earthquakes, Dedo, my friend. It's love that's the most powerful force in nature. I smile just thinking about her. My whole life I've looked up and wondered what it must be like to see the stars and the moon and the sky up close. Never in my wildest imagination did I dream that one day I could actually reach out and touch them. This girl is an angel. An absolute angel," Chagall said breathlessly, not realizing he had cleared the entire path out to the street by

190

himself. "Gosh, it's hot," he said loosening his scarf and his coat. "You wouldn't think with all this snow it would be so hot, would you?" he asked taking off his cap, letting the mop of feathers that was his hair fly loose in the crisp air.

"No," Dedo said looking at his hopelessly head-over-heels-in-love friend with a warm smile. "You wouldn't." Then, Dedo Modigliani put his hand around his friend's shoulder and, taking his shovel from him tossed it along with his own into the barn, and said with a sly grin, "Come on, let's go get some breakfast in you before you float away."

. . . .

"You know your papa is very upset," Harry Lowenstein told his godchild in a stern tone as they ambled through the Old Town Square that Sunday afternoon. "I haven't seen him this much out of sorts since... well, a very, very long time ago, that's for certain, Channelah."

"Uncle Harry," Hannah pleaded. "I know I should have told Papa I was going out, but you and I both know if I told him where I was going, and with whom, he would never have let me go. I'm almost eighteen, can't I have a little fun once in a while?"

At that last plea however, Harry Lowenstein's demeanor changed from concern to anger. "A little fun? Is that what you think this is about, Channelah, having a little *fun*?" he fumed. "Do you understand the consequences if you don't marry Friedrich, Jr.?"

"Is that what this is all about?" she asked harshly. "I'm nothing more than a spigot to improve your cash flow?"

"That's one way to look at it. Another way, for someone *almost* eighteen, would be to understand what that means. To understand what your father understands, what he's going through. And finally, once and for all, to grow up and understand what that cash flow enables... And it's not just a nice house and plenty of fineries. Nearly four hundred employees and their families depend on their jobs at Kessler Insurance to survive. More than five thousand clients across all of central Europe depend on Kessler's policies to manage the risks inherent in their business models so they can stay in business and the people who work there and their families can have jobs too. And even that doesn't begin to include all the others, everyone from the bankers and the others who broker the deals, to the bakers who sell them their cakes and breads. Your father is not upset just because of a little *fun*."

As the solemnity of what Harry Lowenstein said bore down on her, Hannah took a deep breath.

"No, Channelah," Harry Lowenstein said, his attitude toward her softening. "It's not as simple as when you and I used to play in your study on those wintry *Shabbas* afternoons when you were a little girl. If Kessler Insurance tumbles there's a lot more at stake than wooden building blocks and toy knights in shining armor. When you do something foolish like you did last night, if it should scare off Fritz, Jr.—or worse, if it scares off Fritz, Sr.—it jeopardizes quite a bit more. Quite a bit more," he sighed heavily.

Hannah took a deep breath and looked up, first at her uncle, then at the steady stream of people flowing along the promenade just as surely as the waters flowed along the Vltava.

192

And there, without so much as another word, just a simple nod to her uncle, Hannah Kessler steeled herself, and leapt off the cliff of her life committing to an abyss of debentures, risk analysis algorithms, and Friedrich Kohlmann, Jr..

Twenty-eight

A week later as he approached the Jerusalem synagogue, the newest and most liberal of Prague's synagogues, Marc Chagall could hear the last of the blessings of the Friday evening services being sung dutifully by the congregation. He stood and marveled at the structure with its layers of red and beige brick fashioned in an ode to Moorish architecture with its large, curved arches pointed at the top. High above the main entrance, a giant, golden Star of David with panes of stained glass around it and deep blue mosaic tile studded with a thousand silver stars symbolized the night sky.

He sidled up to a window at the side of the building and, peering through, scanned the worshippers inside until he finally spotted what he was looking for: his beloved Hannah. Wedged between her father and Harry Lowenstein, Chagall watched as they, along with the rest of the congregation, stood for the final benediction.

When he finished, the rabbi lifted his head and said, heartily, "Good *Shabbas*."

"Good *Shabbas*," the congregation replied in chorus, and then, neighbor to neighbor, husbands to wives, fathers to daughters, and mothers to sons, turned to each other and kissed, and hugged, rejoicing in the divine sanctuary of the Sabbath."

As the crowd dispersed and spilled out onto the sidewalks, Chagall made his way toward the entrance. There, spotting Hannah as she approached the doors, he moved toward her until suddenly he felt himself stopped and pulled back.

"Mr. Chagall, isn't it?" Harry Lowenstein said, taking him by the shoulder, turning him around, and pinning him between a wall and one of the synagogue's tall, marble columns. "I thought it was you. I said to myself, isn't that the young artist we met on the train? Good *Shabbas*. Nice to see you again," he said, bobbing and weaving with the young man as he craned his neck in search of exactly what and exactly who, Lowenstein knew all too well.

"Good *Shabbas*," Chagall answered, anxiously.

"So, how are things going for you, career-wise, I mean? Have you sold many paintings yet?"

"No. No, I haven't."

"None?"

"None. Well, it was very nice seeing you again," Chagall said, starting off.

"But, you're doing alright otherwise?" Lowenstein asked, stopping him at the shoulder and looking him square in the eye. "I mean, we wouldn't want someone like you, such a promising, up-and-coming talent to suffer too much for your art, now would we? We are, after all," he said waving a twenty-ruble note in the young man's face, "supporters of the arts here."

"I'm fine, thank you very much," Chagall said, wresting himself free angrily. "I didn't come here for your money."

Harry Lowenstein pulled him in close by his lapel and said, "I know exactly why you came here, Mr. Chagall. And I suggest you leave the same way you arrived: neither heard nor seen. Miss Kessler does not wish to see you anymore."

"I'd like to hear that from her directly, if you don't mind," Chagall said brushing himself off.

"Oh, but I do," Lowenstein said gruffly. "I know your type all too well. And there's too much at stake here to let some, some... peasant like you muck it up. I may not be the one to give rise to your career, but I could be the one who brings any promise of it down. So if I were you I would find a new patron to latch onto. *Good Shabbas*," Lowenstein said coldly, then turned away into the crisp night leaving the young painter standing there shaken and angry.

. . . .

Twenty-nine

Hannah watched as her father held court, as he did every Saturday afternoon, strolling along twenty paces ahead of her on the promenade alongside the Vltava with his cabinet of ministers—Lowenstein, Breslow, and Kohlmann. Just before he reached the Charles Bridge, Jacob Kessler took a seat on a bench, the grandest view of St. Vitus Cathedral and the Prague Castle in front of him, as the others sat down beside him.

Hannah stopped too, just outside the boat house, propping her elbows on the railing, letting the crisp bright rays of the November sun warm her face, while she watched the world float by on flat-bottomed boats and half-listened as her father pontificated just out of ear shot about who knows what.

Listen, Jacob," Harry Lowenstein said, clearing his throat. "We need to talk to you. We think…"

"We're not sure, but…" Max Breslow continued haltingly.

"It would be best…" Fritz Kohlmann stuttered.

"Better…" Lowenstein corrected him.

"What already?" Jacob Kessler asked in a huff. "You think," he said pointing at Lowenstein. "You're not so sure," he said looking at Breslow. "And you say it would be best, or maybe worst," he said to Fritz Kohlmann. "Spit it out already. What is it?"

"We think you should keep a lower profile," Harry Lowenstein blurted out.

"We should *all* keep a lower profile," Breslow agreed.

"Keep a what?" Jacob asked incredulously. "I didn't even know I was keeping any profile, now all of a sudden I have to keep it lower? What does that mean? What are you talking about?"

"What he means," Fritz Kohlmann said, "is that things are changing."

"Changing?" Jacob asked. "Of course, things are changing. Things always change. Get to the point already."

"The point," Harry Lowenstein said anxiously, "the point is, the pendulum seems to be swinging again. And each time now, the pogroms get just a little bit worse. They're coming more often. We've been keeping track."

"Anti-semitism? That's what this is all about?" Jacob Kessler wanted to know.

"Yes, anti-semitism," Max Breslow said. "Don't sound so surprised."

"Ridiculous," Jacob snorted. "You're all out of your minds. This isn't Spain. It's not 1492, there's not going to be an Inquisition. This isn't even the same Prague it was in 1792. Look around you. Are we confined to Josefov anymore? No. And we haven't been for more than a hundred years. This is the capital of Bohemia, the heart of modern Europe. It's the twentieth century for goodness sake."

"Jacob, listen," Fritz Kohlmann implored. "The mood is shifting. Maybe not today and maybe not tomorrow, but something is coming. Something is different. It's no longer just a bunch of Cossacks the Czar sends out to shake us down for some cash. It's not just a bunch of hooligans and street thugs out for some kicks. It used to be that when it happened to us the gentile community would be horrified. They didn't do anything to stop it, most of them, but they were at least shaken by the brutality. Now, little by little, they seem less and less sickened, as if they were becoming numb or immune to it. You can see it in their eyes. If things continue this way…"

"Ah, you're exaggerating," Jacob huffed, but he could see they would not be so easily swayed by their mentor this time. He saw, for the first time, that perhaps, they were right. "Alright. So what do you propose? That I no longer walk along the Vltava on *Shabbas* afternoons? That I sneak into the synagogue through the back door on Friday nights? What? You're being ridiculous."

"We just think we shouldn't be such big targets," Max Breslow explained. "Charity is still alright, of course—"

"That's nice to know," Jacob said sarcastically.

"Let's just keep things quieter, not so flashy," Harry Lowenstein said. "No big fundraisers in castles."

"People know where to find us if they need us," Fritz Kohlmann added.

Jacob looked at his friends and shook his head in disbelief. "I can't believe what I'm hearing. From you three of all people."

Hannah continued to watch the four of them from her perch along the railing. As a wind came up off the river, she pulled her collar up a bit, then put her hands in her coat pocket to get her gloves. She pulled out the left and then the right, but as she pulled it out a small envelope, folded in half, fell to the ground at her feet. Hannah reached down, picked it up, and unfolded it. *To the girl with eyes as blue as the sweet, summer sky,* it read in small, neat letters. She gasped slightly and her heart began racing as she recognized the handwriting, the swift, sure strokes of an artist. She looked up quickly at her father, but seeing the four of them still prattling on, she stood up, and pulled out the note inside and read it.

Angel, she read, her hand trembling slightly. *You know my clearest voice is with my brush not my pen, so please bear with me as I try to express myself in a medium I am completely unfamiliar with, and with tools as inadequate as mere words, to describe my feelings for you.*

From the moment we met you have been in my every thought. From the first rays of light in the early dawn until the sun drops beyond the horizon I can think of nothing but you. At night I lay down on my pillow with visions of you—of us—swirling inside my head. Your smile. The way your golden hair frames your face. The way you make me laugh and forget that such a thing as time even exists. And then there are your eyes, oh Lord, those eyes. They reach down and touch me so deep in my soul, surely what I see is that incredible, beautiful spirit of a woman that is you, my dearest Hannah. One look from you and I am breathless. When I am with you it is as if I am holding heaven in my arms.

For the first time, I understand about the Greeks and their goddesses. When we meet and I see you approaching, it is if you have descended from the heavens just for me. And every worry, every care, every vagrant fear and ill notion that ever existed, disappears the moment you smile to greet me.

With your grace, your charm, your intellect, your wit, and your amazing beauty, you have captured my heart like no one else before.

I know it is but one short week we have been apart but my heart is ready to burst. I ache to see you night and day and can think of nothing else except your sweet lips. I will savor that first kiss, that first embrace, that first night, for eternity and I shudder at the thought of having to wait any longer to take you in my arms again. This time I fear I may never be able to let you go.

The scent of your hair. Oh, the scent of your hair. How it intoxicates me so. With my eyes closed, wrapped up together so close that your scent is my every breath, it is as if I am in midst of the most magnificent field of flowers on the most glorious summer day you can imagine. Whenever you hold me close and the scent of your hair fills my senses, I am blissfully powerless to do anything but savor the joyous, free spirit that is you.

Angel, I miss you so much. So very, very much. I cannot wait to take you in my arms and hold you tight once more and feel whole, complete, yet again. All my love... Marc.

Hannah looked down at the note and brushed her fingertips lightly against those last few words on the page, *All my love... Marc*, then she brought the thin, onionskin paper to her lips and looked out at the castle across the river from her and smiled as big a smile as she had ever smiled in her life.

"Pssst," someone whispered. "Pssst," the whisper came again.

Hannah looked around to where the sound was coming from, somewhere near the boathouse just steps away from her.

"Over here," the voice said.

Hannah looked over and saw the door swing open a crack for her.

"Come on, hurry up," she saw Chagall calling her. As she came close he grabbed her arm and pulled her inside with him. Inside, both their anxious breaths curled up in quick little wisps of smoke inside the chilled room of warm, clear light and the waves lapped quietly against the rowboats all lassoed together inside the shack for the season. "Sorry," he said with his bright, nervous smile.

"What are you doing?" Hannah asked. "My papa's just over there," she said trying to leave, but he took her and held her close.

"I've got an eye on him," Chagall reassured her, pulling her closer. Then he pressed his lips to hers, closed his eyes, and kissed her. He kissed her and it touched her so deep in her soul, it was as if she was lifted off the ground.

When he stopped, she asked, "What happened? Where have you been? I thought... I thought you didn't want to see me..."

"I know what you thought, Angel. But it wasn't that at all. They wouldn't let me see you."

"Who? Who wouldn't let you see me? What are you talking about?"

"Your Uncle Harry. Under orders from your father, I assume. I've been trying to see you for a week now."

"Oh," Hannah said sadly. She took the letter she had been clutching tightly in her hands and put it back in her coat pocket. "Look, I can't see you anymore," she said with conviction. "I'm engaged to Friedrich, Jr., I... love Friedrich Jr.," she managed only half-convincingly however.

"Look, Hannah. You are the most amazing woman I have ever met. Your spirit, your curiosity, the wonder that you bring to the world around you is awesome. It makes my spirit soar. I know you're scared. I'm scared, too. Scared that if I don't paint, something inside me will die. And in that same way, I can see that you must grow your flowers or something inside you will die. I can see it in your eyes. It seeps out from your very soul when you describe your daffodils and your tulips. When you speak to me about the scent of your gardenias, I can smell their perfume all around me. You *must* grow your flowers.

"I may be crazy, Hannah" Chagall continued, "but I'm not stupid. I know how the world works. I don't have two rubles to my name. I can't offer you any home, let alone a summer home, a winter home, and yet another home for reasons that are all too unclear to me. But what's one more home, more or less? I'm in too deep with you now to just let you go and forget about you. I told you that before. Remember? You jump, I jump. I'm not going to stop caring about you just because you've stopped caring about yourself. If you go through with this, that passion, that desire, that fire burning deep inside you that I love so much, will die out. Maybe not right away, because you're strong inside, but eventually... Not even you can hold out forever. And then, what? Where will you be? Where will I be? Where will... we be?" he asked mournfully.

She looked in his eyes and saw reflected there the hope, the energy, the spirit that he saw within her, and for a moment, she could see that Marc Chagall thought he had broken through, but in the end, all she heard herself say was, "I've got to go," and she turned her head down, and walked back out into the late afternoon light, leaving him there, quiet and more than a little brokenhearted.

Hannah Kessler walked away, then stopped and started to turn back. But in the end, she steeled herself and kept on walking. As she approached her father, she heard Harry Lowenstein say, "Think it over, Jacob. That's all we ask."

"Okay, okay," Jacob Kessler conceded. "I'll think it over."

Hannah sidled up to her father and took his arm. "Can we go, Papa? I'm getting cold."

"Of course, Channelah," he said looking at his friends. Then he shook his head woefully and sighed as they walked off together.

As she walked arm in arm with her father, Hannah turned back to look at the boathouse one more time, but Chagall was nowhere to be seen.

. . . .

Hannah looked around the long, rectangular table in her dining room and watched the guests—the usual Saturday night assortment of friends, family, and business associates at her house—as they sat, eating, drinking, and generally having a good time bidding the Sabbath farewell until next week. Harry Lowenstein, Max Breslow, and their wives kept things going at the far end of the table. In between, Rose Ensler held her own with those few senior managers from Kessler Insurance invited to join them from time to time. To Hannah's left, Fritz, Jr., continued to press his case for an automobile factory to anyone who would listen, and across the table from him, his father.

The only addition tonight was Victor Karpacz. As he sat across the table from her, Hannah could see in his face that her instructor was beside himself with delight at being seated in the place of honor. To his left, at the head of the table, Jacob Kessler, the legendary insurance magnate. To his right, yet another captain of industry, Fritz Kohlmann. Karpacz was bursting with pride to bask in such company.

"So, tell me Victor," Jacob Kessler asked, "how is my Channelah doing at the institute these days? Is she behaving herself?" he asked smiling and stroking his beard pensively.

"She's actually coming along quite nicely, Herr Kessler," Karpacz said briskly. "Quite nicely indeed."

"And she's keeping up her studies and her grades in your actuarial class?"

"Well, as you know, Herr Kessler, that's a very difficult class."

"But, there's nothing more important in insurance than understanding the tables, is there, Victor?"

"Of course not, Herr Kessler. But for someone who is just being exposed to them for the first time, it's challenging. After all, it's been barely two months. Let's put it this way: She is doing as well, no, make that better than, anyone just making their way into the world of insurance management and theory. She shows a lot of promise. She has your keen mind, that's for sure. She's always the one raising her hand and asking things, challenging concepts—in a good way, mind you—trying to understand them completely."

"She is challenging," Fritz Jr. chimed in with a laugh, a half-empty glass of wine teetering in his hand. "I can confirm that."

"Well, that's what I wanted to hear, Victor," Jacob Kessler said, not a little sarcastically as he took Hannah's hand in his and squeezed it. "As for you," he continued turning to Fritz, Jr. with a slight smile, "there's nothing wrong with having a strong-minded wife." Then, turning his head to the portrait of Libby Kessler hanging on the wall behind him, he asked, "Is there?"

"Here, here. To strong-minded wives," Fritz, Jr. said, then he tossed back the last of the wine in his glass.

"Well, then, shall we repair to the sitting room for some coffee and dessert?" Jacob asked. "Yes," he declared, answering himself. "Ladies and gentlemen," he continued, tapping a knife on his wine glass, "Dessert and coffee in the sitting room."

And again, as though the king had given a royal command, Hannah watched as they all stood and poured out of the dining room and into the large parlor beyond, the buzz of their conversation hovering along above them as though it were a hive of bees.

Following slowly behind, Hannah Kessler held herself back, pausing just before the doorframe and leaning up against it. She reached for the switch and dimmed the lights. Then she just stood there in the dark, watching them all, chirping and chattering on and on about this useless piece of blather and that. The noise swirled and echoed inside her head as if piercing her brain until finally, she could take it no more and she squeezed her eyes shut tight and pressed her hands to her ears to drown it all out.

After a minute, a pair of hands gently removed Hannah's hands from over her ears and a voice from behind her softly said, "It'll be okay. You'll see."

Hannah turned to find her aunt, Rose Ensler, the moonlight sparkling in her soft brown eyes, her sweet smile wide across her pale, smooth skin. She looked up at her aunt as a single tear welled up in her eye and then slowly drizzled down her cheek. "Oh, Aunt Rose, What am I going to do?" she said collapsing into the old woman's arms. "What am I going to do?" she sobbed.

Rose Ensler held her niece close for a good long time, softly stroking hair. Then pulling herself away from Hannah and taking her by the shoulders she said in a low voice, "There's only one thing you *can* do. Follow your heart. Just follow your heart."

Rose looked at Hannah, then pulled her in close and hugged her tightly. "I know it seems tough now," she whispered. "But it's going to be okay. You're a very clever girl." Then Rose Ensler pulled herself away from her niece and dried her tears with a handkerchief she pulled out from under her sleeve. "Trust me, these things always have a way of working out," Rose said, handing Hannah the handkerchief and leaving her in the dark to pull herself together before she joined the others in the sitting room.

Hannah watched the others from the darkened room for a few more minutes, then as something suddenly occurred her, she turned and ran up the back stairs to her room. The moon lit up the room in a pale, bluish white light. She pulled her overcoat from the closet and tossed it on the bed. Then, looking at her reflection in the mirror above her dresser she quietly gulped, "Oh my," and went into the bathroom to quickly wash up. She dried off, then using just a light dusting of powder and some lipstick, fixed her face. "That's better," she said, checking herself out one more time in the moonlight illuminating her mirror. She hurried over to her desk and, pulling out a piece of paper and a pen from the drawer, quickly scribbled out a note. *Out for some fresh air, Papa. Back soon. Love, Hannah* it said. She grabbed her coat from the bed, then her hat and scarf from the stand by the door and whirled out of the room. She folded the note and wedged in between the jamb and her father's bedroom door, then skipped down the back stairs and out the side door into the bright, moonlight night.

Hannah looked on in silence as Chagall stood, staring off into space. His breath curling out of his nostrils in little wisps into the crisp night air, he watched the skaters gliding gracefully at the edge of the municipal ice rink that lit up the night sky at the center of town every year from the first freeze in October until the first thaw in late March or April. "Hi," she said softly as she came up behind him.

He didn't have to turn around to know whose voice it was but by the time he did, Marc Chagall's eye were eyes lit up and he veritably grinned from ear to ear.

"Dedo told me I might find you here," Hannah Kessler said, her eyes positively gleaming in the bright, winter night. "He said you call it your quiet place, where you go to think."

Chagall didn't say a word, his just soaked in her radiance as if it were a nectar from the gods, and he knew that in a very real way, it was.

"I guess I changed my mind," she said coming around the small fence that ringed the ice. "I..."

"Shhh," Marc Chagall said, putting his fingers first to his pursed lips, and then, gently, to hers. "Do you know how to skate?" he asked quietly, his finger still pressed softly against her lips.

No, she nodded shyly.

"Come on," he said taking her arm and walking her over to a long wooden bench filled with people, young and old, moms and dads, friends and lovers, all in various stages of putting on and taking off their ice skates and sat Hannah down. "Wait here," he instructed her with a smile then disappeared into the crowd.

A few minutes later, Chagall returned, a pair of white figure skates in hand. "Thirty-seven, right?" he said, then knelt down in front of her.

"How did you know what size?"

He didn't answer, just unlaced her shoes, added a thick pair of white socks to the ones she already wore, and then laced up her skates.

"Come on," he said, pulling her up onto her wobbly legs and guiding her onto the ice. "Stay with me now." Chagall wrapped one arm around Hannah's waist and the other firmly beneath the elbow, then he pushed them off across the smooth surface with one solid stroke from his powerful legs, and then another, and another.

After a minute, when the apprehension left her face, Hannah began to smile.

"That's it, relax. Get a feel for the ice. Uh huh, like that. You've got it," he encouraged as her shoulders loosened and her smile grew wider and wider.

"This is wonderful," Hannah laughed gleefully as they sailed around the rink together, the wind blowing through her hair, her eyes sparkling like two bright blue diamonds in the clear night sky making even the stars pale by comparison.

As they glided to a stop along the fence, Chagall said, "Now, try it on your own."

"Oh, no," she pleaded, holding on to his arm.

"You'll be fine. I'll be right behind you. I will *always* be right behind you," he said in a strong, clear voice.

And so, in short, faltering steps, Hannah pushed off and started down the ice.

"You're a natural. That's it," he shouted as he skated in behind her.

Hannah kept at it, instruction by instruction, until she finally glided along on her own, her face one big grin. Until that is, with the fence rapidly approaching, she realized she didn't know how to stop. "How do I stop?" she yelled.

"Put the front tip of one of your skates down," he shouted.

"What?" she asked, beginning to panic.

Chagall moved to get ahead of her. "Your skate, put the tip of your skate down," he tried again, but it was too late. Diving down, he caught her, sliding underneath just in time to cushion her fall and, wrapped in his arms, they slowly slid into the fence and laughed until they were in tears. Finally, breathless, lying there on the ice wrapped up in each other's arms, Marc Chagall pressed his lips to Hannah's and kissed her with all his heart and soul until it

210

felt to them both as if they were one spirit, whole and complete in the universe.

Energized, Chagall pulled her up and said with a big smile, "Come on, I want to show you something." Then skating around behind her, he put his hands squarely on each side of her small waist and pushed them both off down the ice. He pushed and pushed, one powerful stroke after another until they were speeding along at a good clip. "Close your eyes," he whispered into her ear.

"What?" she asked, looking back.

"Do you trust me?"

Hannah turned her head back toward Chagall and said without hesitation, "I trust you," she said. Then she pressed her eyes shut and her lips curled up in a wondrous smile of anticipation.

"Hold on," he said. Then, as if she were light as a feather, he lifted her high into the air with his powerful arms. "Spread your wings," he told her. And like the angel that she was, Hannah Kessler did and they skated off through the gate in the fence and down the frozen Vltava beyond, where Hannah soared through the starry night squealing with joy in the sheer delight of it all. "I'm flying! Wheeeeeeeeee......"

When they finally stopped under the clear moonlight, the stars glittering above them by the thousands, Marc Chagall took Hannah in his arms and kissed her again, this time with a kiss so full of the heady magic and intoxicating power of love that Hannah was lifted to a place she'd never been before.

Thirty

"Is this proper?" Chagall asked more than a little nervously as they entered the room, moonbeams spilling through the windows in great, big, bluish-white shafts of light.

"Of course, silly," Hannah answered. "This is just the upstairs parlor, it's not my bedroom or anything."

"Wow, look at all these flowers."

"My mother always kept fresh flowers in every room of the house. Lavender and lilies were her favorites," she explained. "Since she passed away, Papa doesn't do the whole house, but he does keep this room filled. It was her favorite."

"I can see why, it's a great room," Chagall said running his hand along the top of an inlaid mahogany table and observing the rest of the richly appointed furnishings. "And the light, the light's magnificent in here. Speaking of your father…"

"He's never made it to bed before two on a Saturday night as far back as I can remember," she explained, turning on a lamp.

As the light came on, Chagall caught sight of a painting, a nude floating on the wall above the sofa and gasped, "Oh my god. A Vermeer. Is it…real?"

"Of course, silly," she said sidling up to him with a sly smile. After a moment, she whispered in his ear, "Marc… I want you to paint me."

212

"Sure," he answered casually, his attention still turned to the masterpiece.

"Here in this room. With these flowers," she purred.

"Alright."

"Now," she said in a velvet voice, her eyes locked onto his. "Just me... and these flowers... nothing else," she cooed slyly.

"Excuse me? What?" Chagall asked in disbelief. "You want me to do what?"

"Like her," Hannah Kessler whispered, pointing at the Vermeer. "Can you do that?"

"Sure, but...my things."

"Open that cabinet," she directed him toward an armoire in the corner. "Papa fancies himself something of an artist. That's why he was so cold about your work. He was jealous, compared to your work, he's an amateur."

"Well," Chagall said looking inside the chest, "he may be an amateur, but he's a well-stocked amateur."

"Set up what you need," Hannah told him. "I'll be right back," she added with a smile.

"Sure," he answered her, still a bit hesitant. Then Marc Chagall took a deep breath and stood there for a moment, looking around, soaking in his good fortune with a big grin. And with that, the painter set to work pulling together his things—an easel and canvas, a palette, brushes, and a dozen or so tubes of oil paints. Then, sizing up his options, he began arranging his scene. He pushed the love seat around in front of the fireplace and then gathered some of the flowers and other small pieces to accent the setting. When he was done he heard the door open and turned to see Hannah enter in a sheer, black, silk, floor-length penoir and Marc Chagall's jaw dropped.

Hannah stood in the doorway for a moment letting him soak her in. Then she dropped the lingerie to her feet and stepped over to the love seat curling up in one corner, tucking her legs in just beneath her. "Why, Mr. Chagall," Hannah said with a little giggle, "I do believe you're blushing. I doubt Mr. Vermeer would have blushed that way."

"He wasn't looking at what I'm looking at," Chagall said, half grinning and completely paralyzed by her sheer, awesome beauty. Pulling himself together he handed her a bouquet of flowers and stepped back. "Lean a little more that way, no, yes, that's it. No, put your hand back where you had it," he said and walked back to the canvas. "That's it. Tilt your head down, bouquet up just a little to your left. Good. Now, sit as still as you can," he said taking the palette and brush up in his hands. He turned off the lamp, letting her bathe in the bright moonlight. "Keep looking at me, straight at me," he told her and then, as if in a trance, threw himself into his work.

Her eyes sparkling in the clear, white light, Hannah Kessler watched with a sly, quiet smile as the artist dabbed and stroked at the canvas in a zealous fervor until, finally, an hour or so later, he laid the brush and palette down, and smoothed his wild hair back with his hand. "There," he said with conviction.

"Can I move now, Herr Rembrandt?"

"Yes."

"Well, I don't want to," Hannah said, bundling up tighter against herself. "I don't ever want to get up. I want to stay here and

breath in this air and soak in this moonlight and this moment...
forever."

"Oh, you're one of those who can live on air and
moonlight, are you?" he said kneeling down beside her. "Then,
you my dear, will indeed have no trouble making your own way in
this world, for those things are free. The rest of us poor souls,
however," he added with a wry grin, "are addicted to some of the
more expensive things in life—food, drink, the occasional truffle,
or two." With that, he got up walked back to the painting and
picked it up to show Hannah what she inspired. "Do you... like
it?" he asked in a soft, shy voice.

When Hannah saw what he had done, she gasped quietly.
"It's... it's beautiful."

"You... are so beautiful," Chagall whispered back. Then
he inscribed his name and the year in a flurry of brush strokes in
the lower corner of the canvas. Then he turned and kissed Hannah
again, long and hard.

"I... don't know what to say. No one's ever done
anything like this... given me anything like this before."

"I want the whole world to see the love and the beauty I
see inside those incredible eyes of yours. If everyone could see
what I see, there would be eternal peace on earth, I swear."

As Hannah was about to answer, she heard the back
doorknob turning downstairs and her father's booming voice just
beyond it.

"I keep those things up here for safekeeping, Fritz," she
heard her father say.

"Hurry, out this way," Hannah said, pushing him toward
her room, and scooping up the penoir from the floor.

"What about my things?" Chagall asked as he scurried out.

"Just go, I'll get them," she hissed. "There's a small stairway on the other side of my bath, it's the servant's stairs. I'll meet you out front in a few minutes," she said kissing him as she pushed him out the door. Then Hannah raced around the room, picking up everything—the paints, the brushes, the easel—and stuffed them back inside the chest. As she heard her father approaching she snatched up Chagall's hat and coat and headed toward her room. Realizing she had forgotten the portrait, Hannah darted back and picked it up, scooting out the door to her room and closing it just ahead of her father's entrance through the other door.

"Hannah, is that you?" Jacob Kessler asked quietly. "Just a minute," he told Fritz Kohlmann. Then, walking over to Hannah's door, he opened it slowly and peeked inside. As the light from the sitting room spilled into Hannah's bedroom, Jacob Kessler could see her lying there under her blankets, and he quietly, pulled the door shut.

"It was nothing, let's have a brandy," Hannah heard her father say, at which she leapt out of bed, grabbed her hat and coat, and slipped down the back stairway and out the side door.

She pulled on her hat and coat and found Chagall waiting for her underneath the street lamp.

"Is everything okay?" Chagall asked nervously.

"It will be. Hold me close," Hannah Kessler said. Then, wrapping her arms around his waist she closed her eyes and nuzzled into his strong, soft shoulder, his cool, clean scent absolutely intoxicating, and she floated there, completely unaware of time or space, an angelic smile on her face.

After a while, Chagall pulled himself away and said, "I know what you need. Come on," he said, and giving her a small peck on the lips, he took her hand and set off with her into the night.

Outside the barn beneath his loft, Chagall pulled open the stable door. "Wait here," he whispered then went inside.

Hannah listened as the horses stirred inside the barn and then watched as a palamino stallion, its shiny blonde mane glistening in the moonlight, came out of the barn pulling a snow sleigh with Chagall in the driver's seat, top hat cocked just right, reins in hand. The sleigh slid up beside Hannah and Chagall pulled the animal to a stop with a gentle tug of the reins.

"Whoa," Chagall said, jumping down, removing his hat, and bowing at the waist in one swift move. He held out his white-gloved hand and helped Hannah onto the seat, then hopped up beside her and took the reins. "Where to m'lady?" he asked.

As the palomino started off, Hannah looked up and answered. "To the heavens above," she said dreamily. "To the heavens above...."

. . . .

III

Thirty-one

"That was the last time Hannah saw Chagall, or her father, alive," Miriam Reich said as she slowly pressed the book shut, rubbing her frail fingers gently back and forth across the front cover. "Jacob Kessler was killed, along with twenty-three others, in a pogrom the next day,"

"Oh my God," Katie McBride gasped.

"It wasn't supposed to happen to someone like Jacob Kessler," the old woman sighed. "He thought he was immune. We thought he was immune. The Tsar protected some of his Jews—the ones he needed to keep his power—the bankers, rail barons, shipping magnates. But Jacob was in the wrong place at the wrong time," Miriam Reich said in a low voice. "They beat him to death as he was walking to lunch."

"That's awful," Katie said shaking her head. "I don't understand why people do such things?"

"Why? Who knows why?" Miriam lamented, looking upward for an answer she knew would never come. "Jacob was going to die soon anyway, we found that out after. He only had a few months to live. That's why he was so concerned about marrying Hannah off," she sighed. "After the funeral, Hannah had to go straight back home and take over the business. The next day Chagall got word from his friend, Viktor Mekler, he had been accepted at La Palette academy and if he didn't get to Paris immediately he would lose his place there.'

"Did they ever catch the people who did it?" Katie wanted to know. "What did the police say?"

"Catch them? The police?" Miriam asked incredulously. "Are you kidding? Most of them *were* the police. Terrorizing Jews was a fully sanctioned sport back then."

"Sanctioned?"

"By the Tsar himself."

"And what about Fritz, Jr.? Did she…"

"No, thank God, no," Miriam Reich said with a smile. "Fritz, Sr. was seeing another woman, you know, a mistress. When he found out she was pregnant—and Fritz, Jr. was the father no less—he shipped them both away to Ekonda."

"Where?"

"Siberia," Miriam explained, smiling. "The marriage was called off, just like that," she said patting her hands together. "Hannah took over the business, with help at first from Harry and Max and Rose. Then, she met Yossi, Josef Rosen. They got married in 1913, maybe 1914. It was an unusual marriage, especially in those days, but it worked. She ran the business and he stayed home with the three kids, Sammy, Jacob, and of course… Lilly. See," she said, picking up the copy of the family photo Kate had brought from the museum. "Here's the feather duster," she pointed out on the picture with her wrinkled, crooked finger. "Right next to Yossi's chair. You see it there, tucked behind him? He did all the cleaning and cooking and raised the three kids."

"They did very well,' Miriam Reich continued. "But they lived modestly, because they gave so much to charity. So much.

219

Most people had no idea how much Hannah and Yossi gave," she sighed. "Poor, sick, whether you lost everything in a fire, it didn't matter. Yossi and Hannah gave, but always quietly, through the back door, never the front," she smiled.

"So things were alright then?" Katie asked.

"For a while. Until Mr. Hitler came along in 1933. He began by banning certain books and burning them, especially books by Jewish authors. Then the Nazis declared themselves the only legally accepted political party. They passed a law to, quote unquote, purify the race. Can you imagine this kind of thinking? They began to sterilize the mentally ill, the deaf, the blind, anyone they considered inferior. Then they began to point to us as the cause of all their problems. We had to be dealt with. They outlawed doing business with Jewish-owned businesses. People were afraid to even order from a Jewish mail order catalog in case the mailman saw a package coming from a Jewish mail order house and they would be taken away and shot.

"Later that year, Jews were banned from politics, from marrying non-Jews, and even from employing non-Jewish women under the age of forty-five. We were banned from streetcars, from the railway stations. We were banned from washing our clothes in German laundromats. We were even banned from buying flowers. Can you imagine? Flowers. In 1938, the German government passed a law allowing insurance companies to withhold payment of claims to Jews. Then, Goering confiscated all those payments for the Third Reich. Some of those claims aren't settled, even today, sixty-some years later. The insurance companies defended their actions by claiming they were just following the law at the time. Or they asked for documents and records they knew were destroyed in the war even though people had account numbers and other information only they could have known. Anyway, when they took all the money in 1938, that was the end. Kessler Insurance was finished.

"But even when we were in the ghetto and the camps, Hannah was always giving to others, whatever she had; some bread for an old woman, her soup for a sick man. But she wouldn't take anything from anybody. People wanted to help her when they finally found out how much she and Yossi had given to the community, but all she ever said was, 'You keep it, dear.' No matter how little she had or how badly she was hurting, from Hannah, it was always just 'You keep it, dear.'"

Kate listened as the words echoed in the tiny kitchen.

"Hitler marched into Poland on September 1, 1939. One week later we were rounded up and put in the ghetto. From there," Miriam explained quietly, "they split us up. All families were split up. Yossi went to Thereisenstadt, Hannah to Buchenwald. Lilly to Maidenek, Jacob and Samuel to Auschwitz and Dachau. Yossi wasn't well when he went in. He didn't last two months in the ghetto. Hannah died half a year later. Jacob died in the uprising in Warsaw. Samuel made it to liberation, but he died from typhus a week later. Only Lilly survived."

"Do you know how the painting got into the book?" Katie asked.

"Book? What book?"

"I found the painting in the spine of this book," she explained as retrieved it from her bag in the other room. "In here," she said handing *Die Zulassung* to Miriam.

"Well, I don't know exactly," the old woman admitted. "But I have a pretty good idea. Have a little more tea," she said filling up Katie's cup. "Whatever wasn't destroyed was Aryanized."

"Was what? What's that, Aryanized?" Kate asked.

"The Nazis passed a law that said whatever belonged to Jews really should belong to them, the so-called Master Race, the Aryans. Everything and anything of value—silverware, jewelry, art, businesses, doctor's offices, real estate, everything—was Aryanized. Confiscated. Stolen. Looted. However you want to say it. They came to Hannah's house like they came to all our houses in the middle of the night with the guns and the big lights glaring and the barking dogs. I remember it as if it was yesterday..."

"*Raus! Raus, Juden!*" the soldiers shouted, their weapons pointed at Hannah, Yossi, and the teenage children at their side. Next to them, the German shepherds and Dobermans straining their leashes, shrieking into the night, their black eyes filled with bloodlust. "You won't need that where you're going," one of them said to Yossi, knocking a bag full of family pictures and papers out from under his arm with the butt of his rifle. "Out in the street with the rest of the garbage," another shouted. "Now, Jews! Now!"

Hannah pushed her family along. "Go ahead children, it's going to be alright. Everything will be alright," she said trying to calm them. "We're coming, we're coming," she shouted, her hands held up. But as she took the last step down onto the street, Hannah lost her footing and fell to the ground. "I'm okay," she said, picking herself up, and as she did, she managed to grab one family photo out of the gutter and stash it in her pocket. She moved toward the street, by now filled with people marching at gunpoint by the thousands in the harsh spotlights the soldiers had brought with them.

As she reached the gate of her front yard, Hannah turned back to look at her house and watched as another group of soldiers laughing and joking, carried out her furniture, her lamps, her chairs, her tables, and loaded them onto the waiting trucks.

"Hey, Heinrich, check this out," one of soldiers shouted as he held up Hannah's portrait waving it back and forth with a cat call.

Hannah turned to look back but she felt the barrel of a rifle poke her hard in the ribs. "Move," a soldier yelled and she watched as her painting was carted off along with a vase and her golden candelabra. She knew then and there things would not be alright. She could feel it deep down inside. They would not be coming back to this house ever.

"*Shma Yisrael*," Hannah began praying under her breath, "Hear O' Israel! The Lord is our God, the Lord is one!" she prayed. "Dear God, please keep us safe under your wing and if we get separated, reunite us again." She looked at her children and pushed them along. "It'll be okay," she repeated weakly, then she put her hand in Lilly's coat pocket, tore apart the lining, and slipped the photo inside.

"There were so many of them," Miriam Reich explained. "Tanks, dogs, soldiers, the whole thing was over in ten minutes. They locked us in a basement for five days. There must have been five hundred of us in a space no bigger than this apartment. No food, no water, no place to go to the bathroom. No light even. One by one they emptied the basements and began assigning us to apartments, twenty and thirty of us, one, and sometimes two, families to a room. The first orders came the next day: we should send our leaders out to talk to them, our rabbis, our teachers, our strongest men, which we did. They were shot immediately and left to rot on the street along with orders to shoot to kill anyone who should move them, let alone try to bury them. Why, we asked? What did they do? Why them? Every week, they tightened the noose and took more of us away. Orders for two thousand to report, then three thousand more... Every week there were fewer and fewer of us, still, always there was the question... 'Why?'"

"We were the one of the last to go in June, 1942, Lilly and me, to Thereisenstadt. The whole time we were in the ghetto we would get postcards from there saying how nice it was, how they played music, great symphonies, outdoors. But of course, when we got to the camps it wasn't like that at all. The only music came from the gypsy women they forced to play naked in the bitter cold. The louder the screams from the gas chambers, the louder they were forced to play. After that, there wasn't much to say.

The old woman drew in a small, shallow breath. "In the camps, there was only talk the first few days you were there. After you understood what was going on, there's not much to say. You no longer asked 'Why?' You were too hungry. Your last thought at night was hunger, your first thought in the morning was hunger.

224

"There were a lot of prayers. Not much else. And after a few months not even that, you were just saving every ounce of strength for the next breath and cursing yourself for doing so. Some people couldn't take it anymore and they threw themselves against the electric fence. And some of us... envied them. We actually envied the dead, because at least for them the suffering was over.

"One day, I don't know how long I was there, I saw my face reflected in the soup they gave us—soup, ha, warm water and salt. I saw myself there for the first time in I don't know how long, nine months, maybe a year. And my eyes, my eyes were bulging from head and my bones were poking out through my skin. I didn't do that ever again.

"One night when we were marching—they always marched us at night and hid us in the woods during the day—one night, I passed my brother marching in the other direction. We knew not to say anything to each other, but when I saw him, it was like looking at a ghost. His eyes were empty, completely empty.

"But you asked me about the painting," the old woman said. "Because Lilly was so light, with the blonde hair and the blue eyes, they let her clean the offices in the camp. The commandant didn't want to have to see anyone who looked too Jewish, so only the blondes could work near the officers. She was cleaning the office one day and she saw her mother's painting on the wall. When they knocked the satchel from Josef's arm the night they took us away, that was the only photo she had as far as Lilly knew. She had nothing left from her family, no pictures, nothing. When she saw the painting, she went to take it back, what she thought was the only picture left of her mother in the world. But they caught her and the next day they put her on trial and convicted her of stealing. Stealing her own painting."

"Didn't she tell them it was hers, that it was her mother?"

"If she told them that, not only would the punishment have been worse, but for spite they would have done something to it, wiped their behinds with it or something disgusting like that. Then they would have destroyed the painting in front of her or make her destroy it in some humiliating way."

"The court clerk or someone else at the trial probably put it inside the book so they could take it home for themselves. They all took things for themselves. How the book got here to America, I don't know. Probably an American soldier brought it back as a souvenir and didn't know what was inside.

"What happened to Lilly after that?" Kate asked, then looking up the kitchen clock on the wall added, "Oh my gosh, look how late it is. I'm so sorry. I didn't mean to take up so much of your time. I can come back another day.

"*Zetz*. Sit," Miriam Reich said firmly. "You've got another day, and another, God willing, ten thousand days more. Me, I'm not so certain how many days I have left so let's finish," she said with a warm smile. "You'll have some soup?" she asked. Then, she answered herself, "You'll have some soup," and scurried about the kitchen as she continued her tale.

"Finally, we were liberated. April 12, 1945. I will never forget that day. When the soldiers came into the camps for the first time, they looked at us and they threw up. That's how bad we must have looked. We were ashamed of what we looked like, so we kept to ourselves at first. But then we saw, slowly, that they wanted to help us, that they just couldn't believe their eyes. How could they?

We who were there for years and saw it all couldn't believe our eyes. So how could we expect these men, these young boys, to believe what they saw. No wonder they threw up.

"We didn't know what to think. Up until now we had the hope of escape, the hope of survival to keep us going. But now, now came the big question, the biggest question of all, from which there was no escape—*Why us*? Why did we survive while so many others did not? Why did I survive and my sister did not? Why did I survive and my seven year old cousin who had her whole life ahead of her not? The guilt was unbearable.

"We didn't know what to do with ourselves and the world didn't know what to do with us either. We couldn't stay where we were and we couldn't go home again. There was no one—and no home—to go to."

"So, what happened?"

"We waited and we worked, while the JDC, the Joint Distribution Committee the Allies set up, sorted things out. They had a system with quotas, which country would take how many Jews from which place. How many Polish Jews to America, how many to England? How many German Jews to Canada or Australia. I worked in the hospital with the American army and learned how to be a nurse. Lilly worked on the base and learned how to sew. We shared an apartment in Mittenwald and waited to see where we would go. At first they offered Lilly to go to Australia but she didn't want to go there. She was afraid it was too far away to come back in case she didn't like it. Come back to what, who knew. But she turned it down and we came over here together on the boat in 1949. I remember one night the two of us had dinner with the captain," she said with a warm smile. "We felt so special. We never thought we could feel that way again.

"When we got to America all we had with us was the freedom to worship as we chose and the freedom to say what we wanted, to be ourselves. But believe me, that was more than enough. You have no idea what that was like, seeing the Statue of Liberty for the first time..." she said, a tear welling up in her eye, "I'll never forget it... There was a band playing to greet us here too, but all I could think of was the band of naked gypsies. So I prayed. God help me to forget the past, give me the moral strength to be a good human being, and above all, to be a good American citizen."

"Lilly and I stayed with my aunt in the Bronx until we got on our feet. We took English lessons at the high school in the nighttime and we worked during the day. I got a job at the Presbyterian Hospital and Lilly took the job sewing at Beltsman's factory. She took the subway an hour and a half in the morning and again in the night from the Bronx to Brooklyn until she could afford her own apartment there."

"And then?"

"And then, we tried to lead our lives. To be like everybody else. To have a job, a family, to be normal. But normal for us was not like normal for everybody else. We could only fit in so far. People asked what the tattoos were," she said showing Kate the faded blue numbers on her wrinkled arm. "I used to tell people 'We had a big family, we needed the numbers to keep track of who's who.' When they asked what it was like, what do you tell them? That you had to break apart your grandparents' gravestones and use them to make roads for the Nazis to run over? That Lilly watched Hannah go off to a shower she never came back from? That we watched people throw themselves against the electric fence just to stop the pain? Where do you begin? You don't, that's not how you fit in," the old woman said, in tears now. "I'm sorry," she muttered quietly. "I'm sorry."

"It's okay," Kate said, taking Miriam in her arms. "It's okay."

After a moment, Miriam sat up, took a tissue, and dried her tears. "I'll be alright, sweetie. Thank you."

"I should be going," Kate said getting up.

"There's not much more to say. We lived our lives. We did the best we could, each in their own way. Lilly married Abe Stern from the same town back home. She worked at Beltsman's for forty-one years and never missed a single day except when Abe, rest his soul, passed away."

"And no children?"

"No, after what they did to her in the camps she couldn't have children. But she loved them. She adored children. All the kids from the neighborhood knew Lilly. She would stop to play with them every night on her way home from work. Oh, such a light in her eyes when she was around the children..."

"When did Mr. Stern pass away?" Kate asked softly.

"Oh, long time ago, fifteen, twenty years at least."

"And did he have any family?"

"Nobody, that's why the two of them got along so good together. They had no one left after the war but they had each other."

"Well, thank you very much, Mrs. Reich," Katie McBride said as she made her way toward the door. "And thank you for the soup and the tea."

"I hope I helped a little."

"You helped a lot, thank you."

. . . .

Thirty-two

"I'm sorry," the French-accented man on the other end of the phone told Kate McBride that next morning. "We cannot do that."

"But we know who the painting belongs to now," Kate pleaded from her kitchen. "We didn't know that then."

"I'm sorry, mademoiselle. It is the position of the museum that you established yourself as the rightful owner of the painting under the law and we purchased it from you quite legitimately. We have a responsibility to ensure the museum's rights are respected."

"What about your responsibility to do the right thing? This is Lilly Stern's painting. It's her only connection to her mother, a mother's only legacy to her daughter. *They should be together*," Katie implored. "Look, the world already took everything she had away once before in her lifetime, can't we give her back this one thing for whatever little time she has left here on this Earth and then you can have it back?"

"I'm sorry, mademoiselle. There is nothing more to say. *Au revoir*," the man said coldly and hung up.

Kate put the phone down slowly and sighed. As she looked up, she saw Hannah's face looking out at her from the cover of the auction catalog she had framed and hung on her wall. "I'm sorry, too," she whispered softly to Hannah.

"Thank you for seeing me on such short notice," Kate told the attorney sitting across the desk from her.

"Miss McBride, do you realize there are more than a hundred thousand cases of looted Jewish art alone already pending all over the world, including some of the rarest pieces from the Renaissance? Then there are thousands of cases for lost bank accounts, insurance policy claims, real property, all sorts of things," Ann Martin said. "And most of those cases have been going on for decades. Decades," the lawyer emphasized. "For the first fifty years after the war everyone was silent. And if they weren't silent, the institutions claimed the evidence was locked behind the Iron Curtain. Well, they couldn't use that excuse after 1989 so they had to come up with different tactics.

"I was just reading where the Spanish government, for example, refuses to even discuss a Pisarro they've had hanging in a museum there for nearly twenty years. And they've signed four separate agreements pledging to do everything possible to return looted Jewish art and they vigorously pursue their own looted art all over the world. And the ownership records for that painting are there plain as day. Still, their response is 'So sue us. In Spain. Good luck.' And there are dozens of museums more, and the governments behind them, just as cooperative."

"Does anybody ever get anything back?"

"A few people. A dozen pieces or so have been recovered here in New York. The Commission for Looted Art in Europe has returned about four hundred pieces. Occasionally, someone

232

working at museum in Germany or Austria will discover that something in their collection was looted and will do the right thing. But from a legal perspective, your case is very complicated.

Based on what they told you," the lawyer continued, "it sounds like you would need to prove that your claim wasn't legitimate to begin with, which would make their claim—a claim based on yours—null. But if you do that, then you risk being sued, or worse, for having put forth an illegitimate claim when you sold the painting, whether you knew it at the time or not."

"What's the 'or worse' part?"

"You could be prosecuted for criminal fraud, felony. A federal crime."

"But I didn't do anything wrong."

"There's a lot of money and prestige at stake here, Ms. McBride. Don't be so naive as to expect that powerful institutions like this one are going to roll over—or play fairly—to get what they want. This could get ugly. Besides, there isn't even any evidence to support your assumption that if Mrs. Stern were reunited with the painting it would somehow make a difference. Apparently nothing else in her life has these past twenty-some years," the lawyer said. "Look, isn't there something else you can do instead? Take her there for a visit perhaps, have a high quality reproduction made and put in her room?"

Kate McBride looked at the attorney, but the lawyer could tell nothing less than returning the original to Lilly Stern would satisfy her client. "And if we succeed in getting the painting returned to Mrs. Stern in exchange for the money remaining from the proceeds of the sale, you'll have how much left to pay my fees?" Ann Martin asked with a wry smile.

Kate just scrunched up her nose and smiled weakly.

"That's what I thought," the lawyer said. "Alright, Ms. McBride. I have a mother... and a daughter. Let me think about it and see if there's anything we can do that won't result in your having to file bankruptcy or face incarceration. I'll be in touch in a week or two either way."

Kate heard the timeline, clutched the black and white snapshot in her hand and cringed a little.

"Okay, Friday, but that's it. I've got other clients too. Paying ones, no less."

"Thank you," Kate said, pumping the woman's hand enthusiastically. "Thank you."

"Don't get your hopes up, this isn't going to be easy," Ann Martin called out as Kate walked out the door.

. . . .

Thirty-three

"Let me see if I understand this correctly," the judge said cautiously. "Based on newly discovered evidence and information, you wish for this court to invalidate the claim Ms. McBride swore and attested to under penalty of perjury when she sold the painting to the defendants, in order to negate their rights under the contract. And at the same time you're asking that the court hold her harmless for any damages these actions may, or will, cause the defendants, their patrons, benefactors, and the public at large?"

"Yes, your honor," Ann Martin answered.

"And, Ms. McBride is bringing this motion not on her own behalf but rather, for someone she claims is the rightful owner of the painting, the only evidence with which to support that claim is this faded, grainy photograph and the testimony of one witness who can testify competently and one more, the alleged owner, who is incapacitated intellectually and cannot testify on her own behalf? Is that also correct?" he asked in disbelief.

"Yes, your honor."

"Now this may be a gross oversimplification on my part, but simply giving Mrs. Stern the proceeds of the sale is unsatisfactory to you Ms. McBride because…"

"I don't think she would want the money. She would want the painting," Kate McBride said.

At that, the lawyer representing the museum shouted, "Objection, your honor. We've already established that Mrs. Stern hasn't been able to express a cohesive thought in over two decades. Ms. McBride has no better idea than anyone else what Mrs. Stern wants or doesn't want done with the painting or anything else."

"Ms. McBride, how do you know Mrs. Stern would want the portrait of her mother instead of the money?" the judge asked.

"That's easy," Kate said with a smile. "Wouldn't you?"

The judge, unable to find fault with her logic, simply sighed and shook his head. "The parties have tried to compromise and you've been through mediation?"

"Yes," both attorneys answered.

"We would like it known that we tried to compromise by simply having the museum relinquish possession while Mrs. Stern is alive," Ann Martin explained.

"And that was unacceptable to your clients, counselor?"

"We have our rights under the law, your honor. The museum has spent hundreds of thousands of dollars preparing for this exhibition and they've sold tens of thousands of tickets. Clearly, the public is interested in seeing this work and, as we've said all along, we purchased the painting by adhering to the letter *and* the spirit of all the applicable laws, domestic and international. No one tried harder than the defendants to find any legitimate claimants to the property to ensure due diligence had been done— full-page newspaper ads on five continents, the Internet, gallery postings, auction houses, searches of every known art history database, public and private. Even the Commission for Recovered Art here in New York and the Commission for Looted Art in London claimed no knowledge about this painting."

"Very well, then," the judge said. "Let's proceed. Even with Mrs. Reich's testimony to corroborate that the 'Girl with Flowers' is indeed Mrs. Stern's mother, and that the artist himself gave her the portrait, that, in and of itself, does not establish Mrs. Stern's ownership. Her mother might have left it in her will to one of her other children or to someone else in the family. Or to someone else we're not aware of, just as we were not aware of the existence of Mrs. Stern and Mrs. Reich, or the existence of this photograph before recent events. In the absence of any written documents to substantiate the claim of ownership by Mrs. Stern, we would need someone who actually heard her mother say to whom the painting belonged or at the very least someone who heard Mrs. Stern establish her claim to the painting by saying something like, 'That's mine,' or 'That's my painting.'"

"Your honor," Ann Martin pleaded.

"Where are we going to find someone like that?" Kate asked.

"I don't know, Ms. McBride. But, given everything the museum has done by the letter and the spirit of the law, I cannot repudiate their claims without it. I can give you thirty days to locate someone and bring them to my courtroom to testify. This case is continued until September 18th, nine a.m.," he said and brought down his gavel with a sharp crack.

"I'm sorry I couldn't be of any more help," Miriam Reich told Kate and Ann Martin as they stood outside the courtroom.

"Can you think of anyone else whom she might have told?" the lawyer asked.

"No. Who was she going to tell? Me, Abe, that's it. All she did for forty-one years was go back and forth from the house to Beltsman's and from Beltsman's to the house."

"Right," Kate said despondently. Then, perking up, she added, "What did you just say?"

"She just went from the house to the factory, back and forth, that's all," the old woman repeated.

"Exactly," Kate McBride said, her eyes lighting up. "Maybe, in forty-one years, she told Henry Beltsman."

"Maybe," the old woman said, smiling a little now. "Anything's possible."

"Thank you for taking the time to see me again," Kate told Henry Beltsman. "This is Ann Martin. She's an attorney helping me straighten out Mrs. Stern's affairs."

"How do you do?" Henry Beltsman said extending his hand warmly. "Won't you take a seat? Can I offer you anything to drink? Tea, coffee?"

"Nothing, thank you," the women said and Henry Beltsman dismissed his secretary with a nod.

"What can I do for you?"

"We're trying to establish Mrs. Stern's ownership of the painting."

"The one you sold to the Louvre several months ago? I read about that in the papers."

238

"Yes, sir that's the one, 'Girl with Flowers,'" Ann Martin confirmed. "Ms. McBride is trying to have the painting returned to Mrs. Stern because she believes Mrs. Stern never would have sold it had she known of its existence."

"That's very commendable," Henry Beltsman agreed. "Lilly should have it, you're right. But I don't understand, what do you need me for?"

"The museum refuses to return the painting."

"They had a valid contract, no doubt," the businessman said plainly.

"Exactly," Kate confirmed.

"Still, I'm not sure what I can do."

"The court recognizes that the painting is Mrs. Stern's mother," the lawyer explained. "But since, given her condition, Mrs. Stern cannot assert ownership herself, and there is no documentation beyond that black and white photograph that she is in fact the rightful owner, we're looking for someone else to corroborate what Mrs. Reich told the court. We need someone else who might know that it's hers. Someone who might have heard her talk about the painting, claiming it as her own, even orally. Did she ever discuss the painting in all the time she was with you?"

"Oh my...." Henry Beltsman said sitting back in his chair and taking a deep breath. "That was a long time ago, ladies. I don't think so, but let me think about it for a moment."

"Take your time," Ann Martin offered as she and Kate watched the courtly old gentleman scour his memory banks.

"No... I don't recall that in all the years she worked here Lilly ever mentioned anything about a painting. I'm sorry. I just don't."

"Are you certain?" Kate asked just to be sure.

"Yes, I'm sorry," Beltsman said shaking his head.

"Well, thank you for trying," Ann Martin said, getting up from her chair.

"Yes, thank you," Kate added.

"You're welcome."

"This is different," Kate said, picking up a glass paperweight with a bullet in it from Henry Beltsman's desk as she got up.

"They removed that from my chest. I lived with that lump of lead not half a centimeter from my heart for over a week."

"Wow," Kate said.

"That's right, I forgot," Ann Martin said. "You were in the war too. Where were you stationed?"

"Well, I don't know that stationed is the right word, exactly. I was in a POW camp at a lovely little facility in Blensheim. I took that bullet my second day out from training camp, when the Germans crossed into Minsk in January, 1941."

"The Russians took quite a beating early on, didn't they?" Ann asked.

"We certainly did," Henry Beltsman said with a weak smile. "I think we lost almost ten thousand men in the first week." As the women left his office, he added, "Well, I hope you find someone who can help you. Sorry, I couldn't offer anything else, but if I think of something I'll be sure to let you know."

As they rode down in the elevator, Kate McBride said, "He's a nice man, isn't he?"

"Yes, he is." Then she added, "So why do I have that feeling in my gut? You know the one that tells you something's wrong but you don't know what it is?"

"I know that feeling," Kate lamented. "I had it big time when I cashed the check from the auction house."

"There's something there, but I can't put my finger on it. I'm an ex-Army brat. My dad's a World War II nut. We grew up with that stuff all over the house, pistols, bullets, helmets, maps, you name it. Sunday mornings Dad gave us pop quizzes—'Name the generals at the Battle of the Bulge. How many Allied troops were in the rear flank at Anzio'—it was a real blast," she said thinking back and smiling warmly at the memory. "I don't know what it is, but something there just doesn't feel right."

. . . .

Thirty-four

"**Dad, hi,**" **Ann Martin said into the phone.** "Yes. Yes. No, I told Mom last week, we can't make it that weekend. Robert has some banquet thing we have to go to from the office," she continued, then listened some more. "Ok, I'll tell him. Oh hey, Dad, I ran into some guy who was on the Russian front when they lost Minsk. Has the nine millimeter round they pulled out of him in a paperweight on his desk to prove it."

"Can't be," Herbert Martin, captain. U.S. Army, retired, said plainly.

"What do you mean? I saw it."

"This guy says he fought on the Russian side, but he took a nine milli slug? The Germans were using their Lugers and P-38s, both of them eight millimeters. The Russians were the ones firing the nine millis, you know better than that, sweetie. So, unless he shot himself..."

"No, he said he spent the rest of the war as a POW at Blensheim."

"Well, he may have been at Blensheim, sweetie," Herb Martin said, "but he was on the outside looking in, not the other way around if he took that nine milli slug."

"Thanks, Dad," Ann Martin said, the wheels turning inside her head. "I'll talk to you next week, give my best to Mom."

"INS shows that he arrived here as Heinrich Beltsman on an Argentinian passport in 1947," Ann told Kate as they sat in the kitchen of her apartment. "He changed it to Henry when he started the business."

"Heinrich Beltsman," Kate McBride repeated slowly. "Heinrich Beltsman... H.B... hmmm, those are the same initials as on the inside of the logbook, huh?"

"Exactly," Ann Martin agreed. "I checked a little further with the Wiesenthal Center in Los Angeles. After the war, the German records were divided up between the Allies. So, some ended up in the west, but a lot of them were kept by the Russians. They've only been released in the last few years, bit by bit, since the collapse of the Soviet Union. Last year, their investigators turned up a list of Nazis assigned to the Trawniki SS camp in Poland. According to the records, a Lieutenant Heinrich Beltsman led one of the squadrons there."

"So, he was there at the same time as Mrs. Stern. And he might very well have known something." •

"Well, he hasn't told the truth about much else, so why not? He probably figures that the more he gets involved, the more likely it is someone will find out who he really is and what he did. And since he didn't disclose it on his original citizenship application, he faces the loss of his U.S. citizenship and deportation back to Argentina. There's been about a dozen cases like this in the U.S. every year for the last twenty years or so now. But with all of them getting on now, there are fewer and fewer with each passing year."

"So what does this mean?" Kate asked.

"I don't know. Even if we report him to the authorities—which we have to do sooner or later anyway—with his money, he'll keep it in the courts for at least five years, probably more. And that doesn't mean that during that time he'll testify, or testify favorably, on our behalf. What's in it for him if he does?"

"He'd be doing the right thing. My mother always used to say that, in the end, people always want to do the right thing. He must feel some guilt."

"I wouldn't count on it," Ann cautioned. "Not from what I've read about these guys so far."

"I'm not counting on him," Kate said with a smile. "I'm counting on you."

. . . .

Thirty-five

Kate McBride watched as Henry Beltsman swore before a courtroom filled with all the players ranging from the museum officials and their attorneys to the auctioneers and their counsel, to Lilly Stern, Miriam Reich, and Ann Martin to tell the truth, the whole truth, and nothing but the truth.

"Be seated," the bailiff told him, and he did.

"Would you state your name for the record?" Ann Martin asked.

"Henry Beltsman."

"And Mr. Beltsman, again, just for the record, you are the same individual who originally entered this country from Argentina as Heinrich Beltsman in 1947. Is that correct?"

"Yes. I anglicized my name, if that's what you mean."

"Thank you. And again for the record, you are the same individual who has recently been indicted by federal prosecutors for having concealed your affiliation and role with the National Socialists, or as it was more popularly known from the period 1937 to 1945, the Nazi party, on your application for U.S. citizenship, is that correct?"

"Objection!" Henry Beltsman's lawyer shouted. "We are not here to prosecute my client with unproven allegations."

"The indictment is a statement of public record, not a conviction, your honor," Ann Martin said. "But, I'll withdraw the question because you're right, we're not here to prosecute your client. Instead, we're here to try to rectify a different wrongdoing, one that's gone unresolved for over half a century now, longer than many of us in this courtroom have been alive. But if you can help us resolve it today, Mr. Beltsman, at least it won't go on for eternity."

"We're here to establish ownership of a painting, a reproduction of which you see here in front of you, with its rightful owner, Mrs. Lillian Stern," Ann Martin continued. "We're here to reunite Lilly Stern with this portrait of her mother, given to her by the artist, one of only two remaining images—a grainy black and white photo and this amazing portrait—of Hannah Kessler Rosen, on the face of the Earth. You recognize Mrs. Stern seated over there, do you not?"

"Yes, of course. Lilly worked for me for over forty years, you know that," Henry Beltsman agreed.

"And you also know that Mrs. Stern has been mentally incapacitated for some time now since leaving your employ and cannot testify on her own behalf?"

"Yes, I was sorry to learn that."

"Have you seen this painting, the original I mean, before today, Mr. Beltsman?"

"Only in the newspapers."

"What about before then?"

"No, I don't recall having ever seen it before. You asked me this once before in my office, if you remember."

"Yes, I do remember that, thank you," Ann Martin continued. "I also remember you showing us that paperweight in your office as Ms. McBride and I were leaving. You know, the one

246

with the bullet slug you told us they removed from your chest and we've identified here in the courtroom today as Exhibit A," she said holding up the glass weight.

"Yes, I'm familiar with it. I look at the scar on my chest every morning in the mirror when I shave."

"I don't dispute that, not the fact that you were wounded at least. But I want to know if you see something else when you look in the mirror every morning. I want to know if you see a man who made some mistakes in the past but who has an opportunity here today to do the right thing. Maybe not to right all his wrongs, but to at least acknowledge them, if not atone for them in some small way."

"I have no idea what you're talking about," Henry Beltsman protested.

"The bullet encased in this paperweight is a nine millimeter shell casing, is it not?" the lawyer probed.

"I don't know, if you say so."

"I do. We've had it measured, the ballistics report is labeled Exhibit B."

"Very well, it's a nine millimeter bullet," Beltsman conceded. "So what?"

"You told Ms. McBride and myself that you sustained those wounds on the second day of the German assault into Russia and then you spent the rest of the war in a POW camp in Blensheim, is that correct?"

"Yes," Beltsman said calmly.

"But the standard issue for German soldiers were forty-five and thirty-two caliber weapons. And in fact, it was the

Russians who were issued side arms that measured nine millimeters, was it not?"

"I'm not an artillery expert, Ms. Martin. And I don't know where the weapon that fired on me originated. Soldiers retrieved weapons and ammunition from enemy dead all the time, it was standard practice."

"Yes, it was," Ann Martin concurred.

"It was also standard practice for the German army to keep rather meticulous records of just about everything, wasn't it? Who was captured, where they were from, how old they were, what was taken from them, etcetera, etcetera. I mean the archives are filled with volumes and volumes of such records."

"If you say so."

"Thank you. A couple of things trouble me, then," the lawyer continued. 'Perhaps you can explain them."

"I'll try," Henry Beltsman said, a drop of sweat beginning to form on his brow.

"The first thing would be that we've checked the POW records for Blensheim and none of them list you as a prisoner there. We've gone through all the daily roll call records, and the admissions records, the medical records, work details, and the discharge records. No Heinrich Beltsman."

"I wasn't in charge of the record-keeping there, Ms. Martin."

"No, that would be Trawniki, an SS camp where you were the records officer from early 1941 until 1944," the lawyer said. "Do you recognize this?" she asked, pulling out the logbook that had tumbled out of Kate's attic those many months before."

"No."

"This is a logbook, or in German, a *zulassung*. This particular one is from the Trawniki camp. Do you see that here?"

"Yes," Beltsman acknowledged.

"It's a list," Ann Martin declared. "Page after page of items confiscated, from whom, when, what, and so on. Diamond ring, R. Saltzman, 10 November, 1940. Gold watch, W. Witzberg, 10 November, 1940. And so on and so forth. And next to each entry, at the end of the line, are initials, the initials of the individual receiving the items on behalf of the Third Reich."

"Alright, so what?" Henry Beltsman asked.

"For the first few pages, the initials read R.H., someone we've come to learn was a Rudolf Hessberg. But here, in December 1940," she said flipping the pages of the book, "the initials of the entry officer change to H.B. Do you see that here?"

"Yes."

"J. Rosen, sofa, two meters, blue," she read. "J. Rosen, candelabra, gold. J. Rosen, and so forth. Do you see that here?"

"Yes."

"And this one here, J. Rosen, painting, girl with flowers.

"Yes."

"H.B. Those are the same initials as yours, are they not?"

"Yes, but—"

"But many people have those initials, I know," Ann Martin continued. "But how many people have your handwriting, Mr. Beltsman? That is your handwriting, isn't it? I mean, we have copies of the paychecks you signed for Lilly Stern for over forty years from the bank records. That's a very good match, wouldn't you say?" she said, showing him the photocopied checks against the yellowed pages of the old book.

"It's… it's a very good match," he managed to choke out. "But it's not mine. It's a forgery."

"Let's assume for a moment," Ann Martin continued plugging away, "that this is not your signature and not your handwriting. What do you think of what this represents? Of taking things away from people, destroying their lives with such vengeance because of their religious beliefs or their skin color or their sexual preference? Do you believe that was wrong?"

"Objection!" Henry Beltsman's lawyer shouted. "The witness's beliefs are not on trial here."

"We're not asking for Mr. Beltsman's opinion on these specific incidents but rather the types of incidents they represent. If we're going to ask the jury to accept his testimony, it's important they understand the context in which it's given," Ann Martin told the judge.

"It's a stretch, but I'll allow it," the judge ruled.

"So, Mr. Beltsman, was it wrong?" she asked, every pair of eyes in the room holding fast to the pale man now shrinking in the witness chair.

Henry Beltsman parted his lips and drily said, "If it weren't true that there was a conspiracy by those Jews to dominate the world, then what happened might have been wrong. But…"

"You know, Mr. Beltsman, while we don't have any records of you having been imprisoned in Blensheim, we do have these, recently released from the former Soviet Union," she said, pulling out some more photocopies. "These are orders from the German high command in Berlin to the Trawniki unit to begin liquidating the ghettos by mass execution. And, at the top of the orders is your name, Heinrich Beltsman. You not only were responsible for the deaths of," she started adding up the numbers, "over thirty-four thousand people, you were in charge of seeing that these orders were executed quickly and efficiently. That's what Trawniki was, wasn't it? A camp to train officers in the rapid liquidation of Jewish ghettos and concentration camp operations."

"I don't know what you're talking about," the old man said angrily as he tried to step down from the witness stand.

"I'm not through, Mr. Beltsman."

"The witness will remain on the stand," the judge ordered.

"As I said before, we're not here to establish your guilt or innocence in the crimes outlined in these orders, another court will do that another time. We are here to try to right an old wrong, to bring together a mother and daughter, at least in memory, as best we can, after more than sixty years apart. We are here trying to do the right thing for Lilly Stern, a woman who worked for you faithfully for more than forty years and helped you, at least in part, carve out the successful living you've achieved for yourself and your family. We're here for Lilly's mother, Hannah, who lost everything she had for no other reason than she was Jewish. We have kept Hannah waiting for over half a century not only to be reunited with her family, but also to finally put to rest the types of prejudice and tyranny and hatred that people like you represent. And finally, we're here so that at last the world will know the true story behind this incredible portrait and the love it represents. So I will ask you one more time, Mr. Beltsman... Have you ever seen this painting before?" Ann Martin asked, then left the question hanging before him and everyone else in the courtroom.

With every pair of eyes in the room bearing down on him, Kate McBride watched as Henry Beltsman thought over his response. He scanned the room, looking at Lilly, then at the others, then at Lilly again, and finally he parted his lips and whispered his answer. "No."

. . . .

Thirty-six

"There's one thing I don't understand," **Kate said,** as she stood outside Miriam Reich's apartment building, the orange-purple glow of dusk settling in on the bricks and glass around them like a warm fire. "If Beltsman knew Lilly was Jewish, why did he hire her?"

"He had lots of Jewish girls working for him," Miriam explained. "He ran a factory in Germany before the war. He probably had lots of Jewish girls working for him then. He was just trying to recreate his past. We all were once the war was over. It didn't matter what side you were on, everybody just wanted it to be like it was before as much as possible. We lost everything so we had to recreate things even down to the social fabric of our lives. So, we formed societies. We went into the businesses and trades we knew. Something to give us some sense that there was something left, even if it was just a memory."

"I don't know how you deal with it," Kate McBride said quietly, "how anyone could."

"When you don't know what tomorrow will bring," Miriam Reich explained, "you live for today. Look, time is so long when there is suffering and so short when there is happiness. I made a friend when I first got to the camps, she was from Holland. Her name was Simcha, in English, it means joy. She said there were two ways to look at everything—positive and negative. And, she said, looking for the best in a situation was always the better way to go. She was right. It was the best lesson I ever learned. But in the end, we each dealt with it in our own way," Miriam Reich said quietly. "This was the life I was given. That was Hannah's life and Lilly's. I know to you it seems like a thousand lifetimes away, ancient history, and, thank God, the further away it is the better. Yes, our world was much different than yours, but still not so different in the end.

"For us there was no right way, no wrong way, people just did what they could do. Some kept it in, some let it out, some tried to forget... but deep down every one of us knew there really was no way to forget. Look, here we are, it's sixty years later, an entire lifetime, and how the world has changed. Still, we are here talking about it, you and I, and not just because you bumped into a book in your mother's attic. Rose Ensler's grandchildren are still trying to recover the money for the land she and Sam owned for the department stores. Others are just now settling insurance claims, slave labor claims, and looted art claims. And yet, people like Henry Beltsman still believe they did nothing wrong, and then Hannah's painting shows up. Do you know why? Hannah is an angel. An angel who shows us there is always hope. That's what hatred tries to do, to get rid of hope. You've heard of Elie Wiesel?" she asked Kate.

"No."

"He's a very famous man, a writer, a Nobel peace prize winner, a survivor too. He said, 'When everything else is gone, the only thing that remains is hope.'

"This experience," the tiny old woman said, "this Holocaust, sits in our lives as if it sat on our shoulders, imposed on us, like the air, every minute of every day, every dark minute of every night. You can forget about it sometimes, but only for a little while. You think it's gone but then you turn around and look, and it's still sitting there, mocking you, haunting you, sometimes even ignoring you... but it's always there.

"In the end, I guess Lilly's way to deal with it was the way she dealt with everything else—by helping others. The way she figured, the more she concentrated on someone else's problems, the less time she had to worry about her own. What would Lilly want you to do with the money? That's really your question, isn't it, sweetie?" Miriam Reich asked with a soft smile.

She picked up Kate's hand in hers, the old wrinkled skin as soft as a baby's, and said, "She's already told you: 'You keep it dear.' If you do the things that fill your heart with joy and love, and share that with as many people as you can in the best way you know how, you will be doing what Lilly would have wanted done. I'm certain of it," she said with a gentle squeeze of the hand. "You will honor her and those she would have you honor: the survivors, the victims, anyone who has ever been persecuted simply because of their religious beliefs, or the color of their skin, or their choice in lovers.

"In the meantime," Miriam said as she looked across the room at the painting on the catalog cover, "the rest of the world has Hannah now, an angel to watch over them. Maybe the love in her eyes and in her heart will guide them, one by one, as they go by looking at her hanging there in the Louvre, until all the suffering has ended everywhere. Just do what's in your heart," Miriam said squeezing Kate's hand one more time, "and we won't have to keep Hannah waiting anymore. Okay, dear?"

Kate McBride looked into the old woman's eyes and saw the love and the strength and the reassurance she needed, and reached out and hugged her warmly. "Okay," she whispered as the tears welled up in her own eyes. "Okay."

Thirty-seven

In the spring, looking out through the front screen door of her childhood home, the sunlight always seemed to Kate as if it were reborn, as though somehow winter was merely a form of hibernation for the sun. The grass slowly went from brown to green with the first rains, the trees sprouted new leaves. And so too did the sunlight seem renewed, rejuvenated, shedding its harsh, wintry white overcoat in favor of the pale, golden yellows that grew brighter and creamier with each passing day.

"This is perfect, just perfect," Miriam Reich said clapping her tiny, wrinkled hands together as she and Connie Perez came up the front steps. "The Mary McBride Children's Giving Library," she read from the sign hanging above the front door. "I love the way that sounds."

"Me, too," Connie agreed with a big, bright grin. "Girl, you done good here, real good."

"We're going to open branches all over the city," Kate said pushing the screen door open and welcoming them inside, a child darting out from underneath her arm, its mother in hot pursuit a moment later.

"Whoa," Connie said as the little one whizzed by, and then, as she and Miriam stepped inside, "Wow, look what you've done here."

With every wall on every floor, from basement to attic, lined with bookcases, and every corner of the house turned into a cozy, designer reading nook, Kate McBride's childhood home had become a place filled with that singular mix of hushed voices and suppressed giggles,, that glorious, melodious buzz that is the sound of parents and children side by side reading together for the sheer joy in it.

What was once a dining room with table and chairs was now a tropical island retreat with brightly colored beanbags the size and shape of giant seagoing turtles where tall tales of derring-do were being spun out to wide-eyed waifs. What was once a bedroom was now a tree house somewhere high in a redwood forest complete with a view to the Pacific and a soft, squooshy hammock in which to lie back and watch it, while wild adventures played themselves out inside the thirsty, curious, young minds.

"I think after Daddy died, keeping all these books around was Mama's way of filling in the void he left. And she always had a book for everyone. This way, we can keep that going. I figure people can just drop off the books they don't want anymore or we can come get them. Other people can come by and take the ones they need. No checking in, no checking out. It just is what it is, something different every day."

"You figured right, girl," Connie said as she watched the families coming and going. "This is amazing."

"And the Survivor's Foundation," Miriam said smiling and clutching her hands to her heart. "Ahh, that's something special. But what you did for Lilly…well… that was perfect," She turned toward the living room where the old woman sat behind a small desk, a photo of Hannah's portrait on one side and a short line of children and their parents trailing out to the kitchen on the other.

One by one, the children came up, books in hand, and presented their selection to Lilly. And one by one, she examined what they gave her, and with a discernible twinkle in her eye said, "You keep it, dear."

. . . . .

Made in the USA